T0283016

HUNGER HEART

HUNGER

HEART

KAREN

FASTRUP

TRANSLATED FROM THE DANISH
BY MARINA ALLEMANO

LITERATURE IN TRANSLATION SERIES

BOOK*HUG PRESS
TORONTO 2022

FIRST ENGLISH EDITION

First published as *Hungerhjerte* © Karen Fastrup & Gyldendal,
Copenhagen 2018
English translation © Marina Allemano, 2022

This translation was made possible through the generous support
of the Danish Arts Foundation.

Danish Arts
Foundation

Library and Archives Canada Cataloguing in Publication

Title: Hunger heart / Karen Fastrup ; translated from the Danish by
  Marina Allemano.
Other titles: Hungerhjerte. English
Names: Fastrup, Karen, 1967– author. | Allemano, Marina, translator.
Series: Literature in translation series.
Description: Series statement: Literature in translation series |
  Translation of: Hungerhjerte.
Identifiers: Canadiana (print) 20220217378 | Canadiana (ebook)
  20220217386 | ISBN 9781771667722 (softcover) |
  ISBN 9781771667739 (EPUB) | ISBN 9781771667746 (PDF)
Classification: LCC PT8177.16.A88 H8613 2022 | DDC 839.81/38—dc23

Book*hug Press acknowledges that the land on which we operate is
the traditional territory of many nations, including the Mississaugas
of the Credit, the Anishnabeg, the Chippewa, the Haudenosaunee,
and the Wendat peoples. We recognize the enduring presence of
many diverse First Nations, Inuit, and Métis peoples and are grateful
for the opportunity to meet, work, and learn on this territory.

Translator's Preface

Toward the end of *Hunger Heart*, Karen, the protagonist and narrator, refers to Norwegian writer Vigdis Hjorth, whose book she is in the process of translating into Danish: "It's a novel, but the Norwegian critics have been busy adding two and two together and are of the opinion that it's autofiction or reality literature...It's clear to them that the text is her own life." But certain revelations in the book have made some critics feel uncertain about the veracity of the disclosures and query the status of the implied autobiographical contract between reader and writer.

The autobiographical genre has a long history, and conventionally the autobiographical contract has relied on the text's truthfulness while allowing the writer to add a modicum of poetic licence. Not so with autofiction, the genre *Hunger Heart* belongs to. It is unapologetically both fiction and factual discourse, both a novel and a frank account of events in the writer's life. When Karen Fastrup was asked by a radio host whether it is true that she, the writer, really ran naked down Ballerup Boulevard, as described in *Hunger Heart*'s first chapter, the answer was "No." The rhythm of the wording fits into the sentence, the writer replied, and hence the description became part of the story. The French writer Serge Doubrovsky—the first to use the term *autofiction*, in reference to his book *Fils* (1977)—might have said that Fastrup "entrusted the language of an adventure to the adventure of language." In other words, the artist consciously created art from her own history and in some instances flouted the autobiographical contract.

However, breaching the contract is not the same as having committed a deceitful act. As a literary work, *Hunger Heart* in its totality is unmistakably an honest account of a woman who has experienced a mental breakdown and survived to tell the tale. The autofictional text is hybrid: both intimately personal and for the most part verifiably objective, playful, and serious, floating in emotional landscapes while being firmly grounded in geography. Like the books by Canadian writers Nelly Arcan (*Putain*, *Folle*) and Sheila Heti (*Motherhood*), *Hunger Heart* is art with an activist subtext.

Thank you to Karen Fastrup for her invaluable guidance through the novel's linguistic universe that often evades normalized diction and syntax. By way of unusual somatic metaphors—related to skin, flesh, blood, membranes, orifices, and mysterious bodily fluids—the narrator attempts to understand the nature of her anxiety and identity crisis. "Also the act of writing feels physical," the author explains in an interview. She can feel her pulse when she writes and transfers the sensation to a verbal rhythm that frequently manifests itself in repetitions as well as dense imagery. Also thank you to Jay and Hazel Millar for their thoughtful editorial work, and to Stuart Ross for his excellent copy editing.

A note on place names: Most chapters are headed by a precise location and time. Apart from Copenhagen and Jutland, the place names have not been translated but in some cases expanded to indicate the approximate geography and jurisdiction, e.g., Ballerup in the Greater Copenhagen Area and Frederiksberg neighbourhood in Copenhagen, where two of the psychiatric centres referenced in the text are located. Names of streets, squares, parks, neighbourhoods, cafés, and bars are sprinkled throughout the text and have likewise been glossed to orient readers who are unfamiliar with the capital region. Place names that end in "-gade," "-vej," and "-stræde" are typically street names, whereas "plads" and "torv" refer to public squares or plazas.

Marina Allemano
February 2022

For Malte and Selma
For Anne, Niels and Ida
For my mother and father

PART
ONE

I can't breathe, I say to the psychiatrist.

I'm a squealing bullet at eye level who doesn't look to see if there are legs under the chairs. They have seated me in front of a table. No windows, so far I get it. Almost possible to touch both walls at the same time should you get the idea of opening your arms wide, which I wouldn't dream of doing. Arms and legs within reach. Once in a while, hands flap around in my field of vision. Presumably they are mine. I ought to get hold of them, but I don't have time now. I'm talking.

I'm not allowed to be myself, I say to the psychiatrist, in that relationship.

Shouldn't he say something?

I look out through my wide-open eyes, and the words come tumbling out of my mouth.

I want a pair of eyes to look into, do you understand?

He nods, slowly.

I'm supposed to be calm and discreet, I say in a loud voice, but I'm not calm and discreet.

The psychiatrist's brown eyes look at me from behind glasses, try to see if you can seduce him!

Finally, finally there's someone who understands me. He hasn't said a word, but I can see it on his face. We are two of a kind, the psychiatrist and I. When I'm in the row house, I can't breathe, the squealing bullet tells him, because in that place no one can understand who the bullet is.   .

The psychiatrist's signals are a bit vague. But of course he can't just tell me point-blank that I'm in the wrong place in that relationship and in that row house. That's not how it works. But I know he's on my side, he would have felt the same way. It's crazy what I have subjected myself to.

I have forgotten to pay attention to who I am, I say.

I'm a rope ladder dangling down the sewer. Rungs connected by threads. It's probably this ladder I began to pull up to street level and flung down on the dining table in front of Jan and his family at dinner three hours ago, I'm this one and that, and here is the whole pack of us, there you go, most likely that's what I said when I slammed the clattering rungs down on the table and ended up here. How can I possibly breathe?

The nursing assistant who Jan phoned from home, the one who said we shouldn't come here, is present during the interview. I don't like her. Not only because she didn't think we were welcome here. But because she can't see who I am. I'm a very civilized person even if I'm here. One shouldn't misjudge me. And that's what I think she's doing.

They admit me, which you can almost always get them to do. We fight over the beds, steal from each other. But we share certain experiences. I know there's a magic word: suicide. With that you can enter the hallowed halls.

The nursing assistant takes me up to the ward. I'm now hers.

It's society's cost-cutting trick to arrange the hallways in such a way that no one with an already shattered soul wishes to come back, it's well thought out. Psychiatric in-patient units are shitholes. What does that make me?

I look for Jan while walking behind her.

We enter a room. Two metal beds. Naked walls. A narrow window high up. There have been cutbacks since the last time I visited someone in a place like this, no covers on the duvets. Or is it to prevent us from hanging ourselves with sheets and duvet covers?

My jeans and my sweater are draped over the back of a chair. Has she undressed me?

Where is my boyfriend? I ask.

The nursing assistant doesn't answer.

Where is Jan? I yell.

She stops in her tracks, turns toward me.

He's gone home, she says.

My boyfriend has left, *hey*, he doesn't want me.

He's gone back the same way he came. I've been delivered with a bar code wrapped around my wrist. It goes without saying that I should be where he is. The squealing bullet hits me hard in the chest. Something oozes out of the hole, I try to stuff a towel in the gap.

I jump past the nursing assistant, out the door, down the stairs, out through the swinging doors, to the parking lot. Taxis are moving slowly under the street lights. They—or the police— are the ones who deliver the lunatics to the place. The drivers' flat colourless faces are within eyeshot. I'm naked. The west end is so ugly, something we agreed on a long time ago, I don't even have to check to be sure. I run out on Ballerup Boulevard, I want to stop his taxi. Access roads have street lamps placed unusually high above the road. White light. Sounds from tires hitting the wet asphalt. And my bare feet.

I run back. I have to collect my clothes so I can get away in a taxi too. The stairs, two at a time. The room. My clothes still hanging on the back of the chair.

The nursing assistant enters.

I'm going home to Jan, I say.

Just a minute ago you complained about him, and now you suddenly want to go back to him, she says. Can't you see for yourself, it doesn't add up, does it?

I don't remember complaining about Jan. It leaks out of my chest, and I struggle to get dressed and stuff my things into the bag. The nursing assistant is brusque.

You're staying here, she says.

It seeps out of me.

You stay here, she repeats.

Her face is unyielding.

I turn toward her, standing straight and strong.

You people have a problem with communication here, I tell her in a determined, authoritative voice.

Here I am, having to be taken care of by a nursing assistant who thinks she's superior to me because I have come through the door downstairs and run around naked on Ballerup Boulevard. I say to her:

Only people who are truly fucked up come here. They should be treated with empathy.

You're staying here! she says.

Is this a case of involuntary hospitalization? I ask. I know my rights.

She shakes her head.

No, right, I say, and pick up my things.

I escape. It's incredible how fast I can run.

But they run after me. Not the nursing assistant. The psychiatrist and a nurse come after me in the parking lot. They keep a fair distance from me, following me around as if I were dangerous. They say things to me in a calm voice. I know very well why they are doing it, they want to catch me. If they don't keep that distance, they risk me getting scared and running off. That's what you do with animals, you sweet-talk them while keeping a distance. Until you've tricked them into feeling safe and then you jump on them. Possibly with a net.

We think you should come back inside, the psychiatrist says.

I point out to him that they have a communication problem on the ward. Not him, he has a very empathetic way of communicating with me, I say. But her, the nursing assistant. The psychiatrist stands still in the parking lot.

Maybe you're right, he says. But I think you should come with me up to the ward.

I stop. Still keeping my distance from them. I stand still. They stand still. They don't come closer. It's possible the psychiatrist can be trusted. It'll be up to me to approach him if the distance between us is to be reduced. He's not going to jump on me. It's undoubtedly a calculated and conscious move on his part. But it works. I think he's good at communicating with me. That's what I tell him.

I'm glad you think so, he says.

I take a few steps toward him. He stays put, his hands in his pockets. Then he turns around and walks into the building. I follow him.

We walk into the room. The nurse dresses me in a hospital gown and gives me benzodiazepines. Then she leaves. The psychiatrist sits down on a chair by my bed, all the while looking at me.

May I hold your hand? I say.

The words spill out before I have time to snap my teeth together.

He hesitates.

Just for a minute, I say. I have to moderate my request. I'm balancing on the edge of civilized behaviour. The presupposition is that physical contact between patient and psychiatrist is unacceptable. Physical contact between patient and nursing assistant may on occasion be warranted.

It's okay, he says, and offers me his hand.

We hold hands.

Unfortunately I have to let go of his hand quickly without achieving the desired effect of human touch. For the squealing bullet is wide awake and hyperconscious of the thousands of thoughts going through the psychiatrist's head: How transgressive can I expect her to be? How do I stop her? Will she eat me? Give her an inch and she'll gobble up a mile. I'm ferocious. I'm not part of the human family, I'm forced to be abreast of things so as not to miss out on whatever I might be able to pick up here and there. I'm a bitch, I snatch up bits wherever I can, and then I'm gone again.

[Sixteen months earlier]
Sortedam Dossering
Nørrebro Neighbourhood in Copenhagen
June 2014

Anne is leaning out the window of her first-floor apartment on Sortedam Dossering when the exterior door slams shut behind me.

You look great, sis! she shouts.

I'm a bit nervous, I say.

It'll be fine!

I hope so, I say.

The small stones on the path scrunch beneath my high-heeled sandals as I walk under the chestnut trees on my way to Kaffesalonen, a café on the other side of Nørrebrogade. I have a date with Jan, whom I found on Elitedaters.

He's standing inside when I arrive. I recognize him from his picture. He looks serious. He's watching for me. I walk over to him. We both smile, kiss on the cheek.

Would you like a coffee? he asks.

Yes, please, I say, and find a table while he joins the queue.

There are mirrors above the padded red benches. I check my hair, adjust it. Although three months have passed since I moved back from Tanzania, I still have a dark dry tan from Africa, and my hair is stiff after spending two years in too much sun. I can see him in the mirror, he's watching me. I pretend I haven't noticed. He's allowed to watch. Neither of us has any idea who the other is.

We have only seen a couple of photos and written a few things about how much music and dancing mean to both of us. I wrote that I have danced oceans of salsa and small streams of tango, and he replied that if I have danced oceans of salsa, he has played seas full of salsa and Latin jazz.

In high school I fell in love with all the boys who played music.

Here you go, he says, and puts the coffee down in front of me.

He squeezes his way onto the red bench.

He looks sweet, a good person, I think to myself. He is calm, serious. I think his mouth is sexy. It is wide, crooked. He has a cleft chin that's also slightly off centre. I want to sink my teeth into that chin.

He's a therapist, and his day job is treating young people who have drug abuse problems.

Have you ever abused drugs? he asks.

No, I say.

We talk about me being a writer. He thinks it's exciting and tells me he has been thinking for quite some time that it would be interesting to be with a woman who is an artist, something he has never tried before. Other women in his life have been secretaries, teachers. But now he would like to try, especially because music and photography are so important to him.

Of course, I say.

Should we go for a short walk? he says later on. Around the lakes?

We get up and leave. Walk around Peblinge Sø and Sankt Jørgens Sø. I feel awkward in my high heels and with the big bright-red shoulder bag swinging back and forth against my body.

After we have completed the round and stop by his bicycle outside Kaffesalonen, he says:

Are we going to see each other again?

Yes, I say, I would like that.

He says:

Tomorrow?

I nod.

Or is that too soon? he says.

No, I would like to see you tomorrow, I say.

Acute In-Patient Unit
Ballerup Psychiatric Centre
Greater Copenhagen Area
19 October 2015

There's a mentor at the centre in Ballerup, a former patient. He takes turns chatting with us, maybe he's some kind of shop steward for us, the insane. I've noticed him. He comes around to me. I'm sitting pressed into the corner of the couch in the day room, my weighted blanket keeping me together. The TV is on.

Why are you here? he says.

He speaks very slowly.

I look at him. Replying seems to be an overwhelming task.

I can't get hold of my boyfriend, I say instead.

He moves over slightly and sits directly in front of me on the couch.

He doesn't answer my text messages, I say, and he won't pick up the phone.

My hands under the blanket lie still, but my fingers rub against each other frenetically.

We had almost moved in with him, my daughter and I, I say.

I'm sure he'll be back, the mentor says.

I pull my knees up to my chest under the weighted blanket. I'm sweating.

The mentor tells me about *his* partner. I nod. I'm not listening.

You have an appointment with the psychologist in a few minutes, he says.

I look at him blankly.

Haven't you been told? he says.

Probably, I say.

The psychologist calls my name. I grab hold of my weighted blanket with both hands and heave it off.

I follow her inside a small room. There are windows in here. The chairs around the table are scattered all over the place.

So, Karen, she says, and leans toward me. We're going to have a little chat about you.

Yes, I say.

Do you have a good sense of your identity? she asks.

I don't like the question.

Definitely, I answer. My sense of identity across space and time is precisely what one would expect from an individual in our era of fragmented modernity.

I speak quickly.

I feel she's watching me with a curious look.

But I've taken an intellectual interest in the absence of identity, I continue. Rilke's *Notebooks of Malte Laurids Brigge*, for instance.

Yes? she says.

Malte is scared stiff of dissolving, I say. When he becomes fluid, an osmosis between him and the outcasts in Paris, the poor and the mad, takes place, after which Malte is banished from the human community for good and will have to wander about and pick up whatever society discards.

The psychologist doesn't say anything. She gives me a serious look.

I better hold back a little. One has to be on guard.

Do you often struggle with feelings of emptiness? she says.

Now I have no doubt about what she's getting at. I know my shit. We're talking borderline personality disorder here. BPD. But I'm not going there. And my head is *not* empty. Believe me, it's thundering along inside, always, in the fast lane.

Do I bang my head against the wall?

Easy now, I think to myself. That's certainly an unpleasant thought.

No, I say.

Do you ever cut yourself? she asks.

I've only done that once, I say, and I was under emotional stress.

I stretch my left arm across the table. There are two small white lines across my wrist on the inside.

Are you sometimes manic? she asks.

I think carefully. That question is not too threatening.

Sometimes I might be flying a bit, I say, and wave my hand in front of my ear. Like, supersonic, I add.

But you don't borrow money and that sort of thing?

No, of course not, I say.

She says all the same:

I believe you're suffering from bipolar disorder.

That's okay with me, as long as I steer clear of borderline. The plebeian diagnosis, that's what my friend, who is bipolar, calls it, it's like tramp-stamp tattoos and big-time self-harm. Diagnoses are categorized in a ranking system of refinement. My great-grandmother was bipolar. Bipolar disorder is at the high end, I don't mind suffering from that.

I'll get you into treatment with Lamictal starting today, she says.

Okay, I say.

The idea is that I have to get up now.

I get up, shake her hand, and say thank you.

Askov Folk High School, Jutland[1]
1969

There's nothing wrong with me, I just lose consciousness. Everything has been checked. Pumps and electrodes, endless tests, but there's nothing wrong. I just cry until I'm burning hot and my hair is soaked in sweat, my mouth an open wound on my face. Then the breathing stops and I lose consciousness. It happens as sure as death, every time I begin to cry it happens.

I arch my back, shatter, scream. My arms are flailing in the air, I'm drowning, drying out, and they carry me into their bed, lay me down and draw the curtains, turn off the light, total darkness is required, the doctors say, no sensory input, not even from people, my mother and father close the door behind them.

I'm eighteen months old when it begins.

Vesterbro Neighbourhood in Copenhagen
June 2014

Jan has found us a little sushi place in the Vesterbro neighbourhood. We drink white wine, and I tell him about my two years
in Africa, about the girls and women of Zanzibar who walked
into the water to tend to their underwater fields of seaweed,
wearing red-and-orange dresses that would puff up on the surface and envelope their dark bodies like dazzling balloons. He
looks at my hands that move in the space between us while I
speak, follows them closely, says they move beautifully.

When we later walk along Vesterbrogade, I know I want him.
It's the way he puts his feet on the ground, the way his shoulders
turn when he walks, a bit hunched. We walk down to Café Mandela in the area of Halmtorvet where Al Agami & the Supreme
Court are playing, and that's where I discover that his body is an
endless field of sensory experience. He reacts strongly to everything I do, his nipples harden under his shirt, and when I touch
them, his breathing becomes rapid. At first I think it's some
kind of hiccup, but it stops as soon as I withdraw my hands and
only comes back when I touch his chest and stomach.

I smile at him and nod toward the dance floor.

Do you want to dance? I say.

He smiles and gets up.

Of course, he says.

We're good dancers, as might be expected, he's a drummer after all. I feel hot. I want to tear his clothes off, I want to feel his dick in my mouth.

But we can't do all that, we have no place to go, both of us have children at home. So the next few times we meet, we go to photography exhibitions. Every time I touch him, his dick gets hard, I can both see and feel it, and he breathes in that gasping way.

I thought you had the hiccups, I say, the first time I touched you.

Acute In-Patient Unit
Ballerup Psychiatric Centre
Greater Copenhagen Area
20 October 2015

We drag the weighted blankets behind us. Or we settle down here and there so our bodies can curl up underneath them. Every day a young man sits by my feet. Things are going downhill for him, it's not hard to see that. He's started to pace. Here we wander up and down the floorboards when things aren't going well. Some of them move slowly, stiffly, as if they were remote-controlled. I walk fast. I dart back and forth. Scratch my arms with my fingernails. They, the nursing assistants, sit inside the glass cage with their coffee and keep an eye on us.

Now and then a certain calmness is in the air. When that happens I settle down on the couch in the dayroom. I send text messages to Jan. Tell him that they say I'm bipolar. Apologize for everything I've done, even if I can't remember what it is. They say I was psychotic the night I was admitted, I write.

But I must have done something terrible since he isn't here.

I send a text to Ida, who's away, travelling.

She answers: My friend, I didn't know you were having such a hard time.

That's because I haven't told anyone, I write.

A man who's sitting in the day room around the corner says hello. The TV is on, always. Hello, he says again, and I can't see if he's saying hello to someone the rest of us can't see.

My teeth stick out of my mouth horizontally, which worries me. I can feel them under my upper lip, they grow outward and upward. Sometimes a nurse comes over and breathes along with me and asks if I see something behind her when I stare past her shoulder. She isn't referring to the other lunatics. The staff are always monitoring us, checking if we've begun to hallucinate. Hallucinating is not a good thing.

The man says hello again, perhaps we'll end up calling him the "Hello Man" in the same way we call the young man who's sitting on the floor with me the "Dumpster Man."

Why do you say hello all the time? one of the other patients suddenly says, angrily, and I become anxious, the Dumpster Man too, both of us wince. We would rather not have too much commotion.

The Hello Man doesn't answer, it's all quiet over there.

The Dumpster Man tells me he understands that they have to do the experiments, but he—and here he sucks in air through his teeth with a whistling sound—thinks the fact they use human beings is a bit, you know...I don't get to hear what kind of experiments they are working on, because now the Dumpster Man drops over the edge we constantly try to steer away from, and he begins to sing while pacing. Actually, now he looks happier.

They take the Dumpster Man away and move him downstairs to the locked ward, and the next day I spot him in the smokers' cage in the garden.

When I lean over the balcony railing, I can see and hear them. Matted hair and backs covered in blankets. There are always cigarettes. They talk more with each other when in the cage than we do up here. They seem to be on friendly terms, attentive, as if they try very hard to make conversations work within the constraints imposed by the cage. There are several worlds and agendas; they are often convoluted and have tentacles reaching all the way out into the universe and inside ducts and computers, it's about threads, networks, everything is connected, unbelievable how all things have a purpose, there are sex organs under the street of Øster Søgade, and television functions as a centre for signals going in both directions. Organs can be teased out of bodies with crochet hooks and pulled through wires you would have thought were too narrow for kidneys and spleens, it's about experiments, and there are many involved. Most of us, in fact, but each person down in the cage has their own network, and the threads seldom overlap, yet they spare no efforts to keep the conversation going.

When I think about Jan, and my children, I start tearing around, up and down the hallways, my feet don't touch the ground, I don't get snagged on the floorboards, and my skin, my skin does an admirable job. I ought to treat it with kindness. However, I'm not considerate to myself. My skin is like a taut, vibrating membrane around nothing, an expanding bubble-gum bubble filling with emptiness.

But I'm listening carefully, that's why I know things. Although I'm not exactly as I should be, I always manage to think that I must remember what I hear, so I can use it the day I'm able to write again—if that should ever happen. That's how I know he's called the Dumpster Man. I heard them talking about it. It was because somebody once found him on the bottom of a dumpster in Sundevedsgade. And then the police drove him out here.

I don't know what my name will be.

Sønder Vilstrup, Jutland
The 1970s

There's a thing I do almost every day: I sneak into my father's study, which is packed with books, German newspapers, blue acrid-smelling mimeographs, piles of paper, the typewriter with the curved return arm he whacks to make the cylinder pull the paper up an additional line, the tray with pencils and rulers. He underlines passages in the books he's reading, but only with a ruler, and he writes comments in the margin and adds exclamation marks, up to three in a row.

When he isn't in there, it's very quiet, and I close the door behind me and climb up on the office chair, which begins to swivel at an alarming rate until I'm all the way up and can grab hold of the edge of the desk. I open the top drawer, push a magazine to the side, and pull out the photograph. It's a large black and white taken by a real photographer. It's of my older brother Jens. His hair is dark, and his long eyelashes are black. He's sitting on his knees, wearing black rain pants. He's holding a stick in his hand and looks at me with eyes that dilute my anxiety.

Acute In-Patient Unit
Ballerup Psychiatric Centre
Greater Copenhagen Area
21 October 2015

Anne and my brother Niels arrive, bringing me clean underpants from Jan's place. Health Services in the Capital Region
have gifted me with a toothbrush. Now listen, they say. But
there's only one thing I want to hear. Since yesterday I have no
body. It isn't a metaphor. I am whatever I say I am. Empty words,
for instance. Anxiety. I'm the thing that tears back and forth in
the hallway. The nursing assistants in the glass cage. They look
at me when I charge past them. The panicky birds in front of
me might be hands, possibly even attached to my arms. The
nursing assistants could at least remove them. The guy who's
facing the closed door begins to rock every time I pass him.

Good Lord, such a hurry! he mumbles.

A text message from Jan was received today: *I have left you,
definitively*. Such a formal word, *definitively*, I've never heard him
say that word.

Anne and Niels take me down to the end of the hallway.

Sit down on the sofa, Karen, they say.

I look at them with suction-cup eyes.

Karen, Niels says. Jan is not coming back, and you can't live
at his place anymore.

My hands fly up to my face.

Then Niels says:

You threatened him with a kitchen knife the same evening you were admitted here.

I get up. I yell:

I did *what?*

That's what you did, Karen, says Niels. He is crying. You threatened him with a knife.

I pace back and forth.

What have I done?

I can't remember anything, but now something comes back to me, somebody deep inside my head is shouting:

KAREN, YOU'RE FUCKING INSANE!

Jan lifts me up in the air, from behind. I hang from his arms. He shouts:

GET AWAY FROM HERE! GET SOMEWHERE SAFE!

Am I a human being you would bring to somewhere safe?

Now I remember a little bit, I say, and look at Anne and Niels, terrified.

Anne and Niels are standing up.

I need something strong, now! I say.

Niels tries to hold me, Anne is running.

It's *me.* I'm the one who is dangerous. People need to be protected from *me.*

I want to be punished. Hanged, drawn, and quartered. With my panties off and tied down on top of the bowl where the furry ones are kept. Rats don't know about limits, they can easily find fleshy tubes and canals and eat their way through them. And me, phobic to the point where I cannot even touch the word rat!

I sit down, rocking back and forth.

I've never seen Niels cry this way, so loudly. A nurse comes running with pills. Anne is right behind her. The nurse's thighs around my own, she's sitting on the coffee table in front of me. Niels on one side, Anne on the other, the benzodiazepines, the nurse around my thighs, breathe with me. Only that, nothing else, breathe. Look into my eyes. You're here, Karen, Karen, you're here. Breathe. What do you see, Karen? Stay here. Am I dying? I can hear Niels crying beside me. And the benzodiazepines in my arms, it feels fucking sweet now, and I understand all too well why they look so intensely at us when they give them to us, benzodiazepines eat the soul,[2] they say, and they hint at a life they stubbornly claim lies ahead of us. We're barely allowed any drugs. It's important that we can visualize ourselves in some future existence. Putting an end to one's life is against the rules.

The nurse and the benzodiazepines reinstall me inside a body. My siblings have different faces now, they are red and wet, and their eyes are really weird, I've never seen them like that, they are busy watching the nurse. I'm not certain what's happening here, my siblings are usually cool.

Dyrehaven
June 2014

On Constitution Day in June, Jan and I take a trip to Dyrehaven, the nature park north of Copenhagen. It was my idea. I have to see him naked, I want to lie underneath him and feel his dick. I'm thinking it might be possible to find a spot there where it can be done, seeing that we have children at home.

Good thinking, he says.

We brought our lunch. The things I brought along have turned into a squishy mess in my bag, I wasn't thinking clearly, his lunch is nice and properly wrapped. We put mine aside and eat his.

I brought two beers.

Do you want a beer? I say.

No, thanks, he says.

We drink his water.

I lie naked underneath him in the grass. His body is calm, I caress his lips with my fingers, right there where his upper lip rises, a bit lopsided. His eyes are closed, I feel the lines on his face against my hands, his mouth is open, I stick my finger inside behind his lower lip and feel the smooth wetness. His lips close around my finger that rests in the dip of his tongue, I pull it out again, stroke his lips. I am dripping, wet and ready. I spread my legs under him.

He stretches his arms out and lifts himself up above me, looks down at himself.

I don't know what's happening, he says. I've never experienced this before.

His dick was throbbing hard every time we wandered around looking at photographs, but now it's limp. He looks confused.

I smile at him. Turn my head and kiss his forearm, stroke his face.

It doesn't matter, I say.

I'm worried about myself, don't understand what it is I am doing to him. I sense it's not because I don't turn him on. Maybe I open my legs too wide, I'm thinking.

Let's make a deal. When we see each other over the next while, you're not allowed inside me, I say a little later.

It was something I once read in a magazine on sex counselling.

Apparently it's working—the next time we're together, he enters me again and again. We lie on mattresses on the floor in the large apartment I borrowed on Sortedam Dossering, above Anne and Mikkel's apartment. Selma is out, we play music for each other, taking turns choosing songs. I roll onto my stomach, my Mac is on the floor beside the mattresses.

"Black Magic Woman"? I say.

Yeah, he says.

He cups my lower back with his hands, squeezes, touches my buttocks with his lips. I tell him about that evening when I was fourteen, lying upstairs in my bed listening to my father and his students from Kolding Højskole play "Black Magic Woman" downstairs. How I was tossing and turning, perspiring and getting wet and miserable, having no idea how to survive until the time when I could sleep with boys and men.

I'm sitting with my children in the room where the chairs around the table are left helter-skelter.

Selma sits straight up without taking her eyes off me.

I tell them I'm sick; I'm bipolar. Try to explain what it is and how it is treated. I assure them that I will get it under control. I'm strong, even if it might not seem that way right now.

Think of all the things I managed when we lived in Tanzania, I say.

She nods.

It's okay, Mom, she says. We will sort it all out for sure.

Yes, I say. I promise we will.

Malte is sitting close to her. He's looking at her.

But there's something else, I say.

Her body and face are not moving, everything is expressed through her eyes.

I take a deep breath.

The thing is that Jan has left me, and we have to move, I say.

I didn't know that things could happen so suddenly, that a face could turn bright red in a split second. But that's what Selma's face does. There's panic in her eyes.

35

I reach for her hands across the table. She doesn't react.

Oh, sweetheart! I say.

Where are we going to live now? she asks.

Her voice sounds desperate.

I'll find a solution for us, I say.

I'm sure it will work itself out, Selma, Malte says.

To start with, we will stay with Anne and Mikkel in their living room, I say. And then I'll find a place of our own.

She looks away.

Can I have a closet for my things? she says.

After seeing them to the door, I begin pacing again. Back and forth at a frenzied speed. Scratching my arm. I have ruined everything. For myself and Selma and Malte. I am uninhabitable. Can't be contained in this body. But can't get out of it either. When I pace back and forth, I get away from it as far as I can, to the very edge.

A nurse approaches me. I try to stand still and talk to her, but I can't. She says she has something to calm me down.

We just have to stop my body from tearing around so we can get the pills inside me. It's difficult but we finally succeed.

Their dope works wonderfully fast, and she sits me down on a couch in the dayroom and gets my weighted blanket and tucks me in.

I'm able to lean back and rest my head against the back of the couch.

Sønder Vilstrup, Jutland
The 1970s

I slide across the ice in my white figure skates. I've given up trying to persuade Niels to stay even longer than what I've already pressured him into. He's small and thin, and by now his lips have turned blue and I'll have to let him go.

The snow creaks as he runs back home. Then the kitchen door closes shut behind him, over there, far away, causing a flock of rooks to take off from the dead tree by the end of the barn. But then everything turns quiet, and my hands inside their mittens hang limply by my side. Black fields and a farm, that's all. An empty expanse caves in on me and I become a tiny point inside myself, looking out through the holes in my eyes.

That's where I am. And from where I destroy everything for myself.

Copenhagen
July 2014

Jan is in Bali for two weeks with his son, Oliver. I'm translating a Swedish novel. I'm happy, I'm in love, I'm writing to Jan. I tell him about the work with the translation, about the dust particles I can see rising in the columns of light in the room while I'm working, that it looks as if they rise endlessly and never fall. I respond to what he wrote to me the day before, about their hiking trip.

His messages are short. I'm not very good at writing, he tells me. It doesn't matter, I reply. It's just me being full of words, they spill out of my fingers.

I stop writing so much.

In-Patient Unit
Ballerup Psychiatric Centre
Greater Copenhagen Area
23 October 2015

I have a roommate now. She's standing behind her rollator.

You don't look like somebody who steals, she says.

That's because I don't, I say.

No, you don't seem to be the type, she says.

But she doesn't look completely convinced. And she keeps her things locked up.

In the afternoon I have an appointment with a psychiatrist. She's wearing a long, colourful hippie dress. I like her.

I would like to further explore the possibility that you're bipolar, she says, and looks at me.

You're not certain? I say.

No, she says. When we discharge you, I would like you to be registered with our outpatient unit here.

My leg is bouncing up and down furiously.

What else could be wrong with me? I say.

In the evening I pace up and down in the ward and all the way to the staircase that leads to the ER Admission and the entrance from the parking lot. When I lean over the railing, I can see the door below. Anne and Mikkel are coming to visit me. I start watching for them at seven o'clock although they are not due until seven thirty.

Here they are, and I run down the stairs.

I look up at Mikkel.

Why do you think Jan isn't visiting me?

I think he's afraid that if he sees you, he'll be reminded of his feelings for you.

A warm sensation spreads throughout my body and I try to convince myself that he is right.

We go to my room.

What is that? Mikkel says, pointing at the weighted blanket on my bed.

That's my calming blanket, I say.

Mikkel picks it up, feels its weight in his hands, and wraps it around his shoulders. Staggers around with the blanket as if he is out of his mind, laughs.

I can't help laughing. Anne too. I want them to stay with me longer.

Have you seen *Homeland*? Mikkel says.

No, I say.

The main character is bipolar, he says. She is supercool.

Let's find *Homeland* on your computer, Anne says.

We find it.

Look, isn't she awesome? Anne says.

Sure, I say.

You can watch it after we leave, Anne says.

My roommate is asleep when I return after having seen Anne and Mikkel out to the stairs She's snoring like a lunatic. I put earplugs in my ears, but it doesn't help.

The next morning I run into her in the room where the cheese sandwiches and the red coffee carafes are set out.

She says to the others:

When I woke up this morning, Karen had her pillow and duvet pulled up covering her head.

I raise my hands, dismissively.

It's okay, I say.

It's very important to be kind, otherwise you don't know what will happen. Not being kind could open yourself up to attack, for instance.

Café Krudttønden
Østerbro Neighbourhood in Copenhagen
March 2015

When Jan is on stage behind his timbales with sticks in his hands and one foot on the bass drum pedal, his expression is the same as when we make love. Only I know this. He closes his eyes. His facial muscles alternate between being relaxed and open with his soft lips parted to being tense with clenched teeth, tightened lips, his head thrown back, his upper body quietly swaying back and forth while his hands and sticks at the end of his arms move, each at its own constantly changing tempo. Now and then he opens his eyes and finds me, looks at me.

I'm on the dance floor wearing my stiletto dancing shoes with suede soles so I can easily spin. Sweat is running down my neck. The guy I'm dancing salsa with stops spinning me around and pulls me in close. My left lower arm hangs over his shoulder and back, his thigh is between mine, our steps are now short and tight, and my hips sway like Jan's upper body. He looks down at me, I look up at him.

Sønder Vilstrup, Jutland
The 1970s

Pride in my father flows through me. He is agile, stands straight.
He was a ski jumper at Holmenkollen in Norway, and he can:
Paddle a kayak and a canoe
Steer a sailboat and row a dinghy with oars and handle an
outboard motor
Use a map and compass and survive in the mountains
Play jazz on the grand piano in the living room
Repair the bricks in the half-timbered walls of our house
Use all types of implements and tools
Read many books and newspapers
Drive a tractor and a truck
Fell trees with a chainsaw
Make a nice charcoal drawing of a rowboat
Help me with all my subjects in school, except for mathematics
Climb ropes and do lateral arm swings
Repair cars because he was a mechanic before going to
university
Skate and do pirouettes.
He was in the Resistance and poured silicon carbide powder
in the Germans' cars. He had a pistol that he threw in the Lim-
fjord after the war.

My father beams when I:

Am funny, cheeky, brave, covered in dirt, tell long stories, recall my dreams at the breakfast table, describe situations and how people look, have wild hair, do a lot of stuff, among other things climb the rope in the copper beech in the garden as well as turn handsprings.

Nordvest Neighbourhood in Copenhagen
June 2015

The alarm clock rings. It is 7:30 a.m. I switch it off and turn toward Jan. I find his hands under the duvet and hold on to them. He strokes my hands with his thumbs.

Good morning, sweetie, I whisper.

He's lying very still and looks at me, smiling, as if we haven't seen each other in a long time.

Good morning, sweetie, he whispers back to me.

We're lying on our sides, holding on to each other's hands.

I didn't hear Selma leaving at all, I say. Did you?

He smiles.

I heard her eating her cornflakes, he says.

I laugh.

Clink, clink, he says, imitating the sound of the spoon hitting the side of the bowl.

Here's a flake I have to catch, he continues, and hey, here's another one.

I turn onto my back and stretch out.

Unbelievable that I managed to sleep through that, I say.

It just feels homey, he says.

You're so good and generous toward my kids, I say, and kiss him on his chest before getting out of the bed.

When we say goodbye at my door an hour later, I feel something erupting inside me. I tense up and feel the need to ask when we'll see each other again. But I know I can't ask that question, and I wish I were like him.

While we were cuddling under a blanket on my balcony last night, he talked about freedom. He often does that.

An enormous amount of strength lies behind a wish for freedom as strong as that, I'm thinking.

What does freedom mean to you? I ask.

Yeah, what does it mean, he says, staring into space.

He looks into my eyes when we make love and when we wake up in the morning. He looks into my eyes when we meet after several days of being apart. But when we have longer conversations, he doesn't look into my eyes. I often feel a sense of longing when I can't hold on to his gaze. At other times it's boredom. Conversations without eye contact are boring.

It's the feeling of knowing that nobody is waiting for me, he continues, pulling the blanket closer around himself. Neither children nor girlfriend. The fact that I, when cycling home from work, can always do whatever I want.

I watch his profile while he's talking and looking straight ahead.

That I can stop and watch some kids playing soccer. That I can stroll around the city taking photos. Or go down to the rehearsal space and be by myself as long as I want.

I nod.

And I like not knowing when we will see each other again, he says. That we agree on a date when the urge arises.

Yes, I say.

And you're also by yourself quite a bit, he says, when you write and translate.

Yes, I also need to be alone, I say.

Exactly, he says.

But probably not as much as you, I add, and rest my head on his shoulder.

Sønder Vilstrup, Jutland
The 1970s

I'm able to accommodate the adults. But I'm not a nice child, I only do it for my own sake, I'm devious, my motivations are suspect, I tidy up and make coffee and light the fire in the wood-burning stove before my mother comes home, it's cold here, so incredibly cold, I prepare sandwiches for her, a pleasant smell of coffee is in the air, and the living room is nice and warm when she arrives. Otherwise she has no energy, she's tired, terribly plagued by headaches and bad moods. That's where I enter the picture. Because it can actually be altered somewhat so that a few scraps come my way and the anxiety that sits in my body recedes a bit.

My anxiety and the look in her eyes share the same bloodstream.

Nordvest Neighbourhood in Copenhagen and Lyngby, Greater Copenhagen Area
July 2015

From time to time a thought jabs at me like a piercing awl: the reason I want to live with Jan more than anything is because I desperately long to get rid of the grating disquiet and tugging in my belly that I feel for him. But when I sense the sharp points boring their way up, I stomp on them.

Besides, he is such a kind and calm person that it's hard to imagine that things could go wrong. We never raise our voices when together. And I feel bad about leaving Selma when I'm at Jan's place. And I think it's a shame that Oliver is left by himself when Jan is at my place.

Oliver is always looking for food. He calls when Jan is at my place and asks what to eat for supper. There's nothing in the fridge. They talk back and forth, and the conclusion is that Jan e-transfers fifty kroner to Oliver so he can go down and buy some ground meat and pasta.

Couldn't you make sure the fridge is always well stocked? I ask. He's usually starving, as you know.

It wouldn't work, Jan says. He would eat everything in sight. When I buy a pack of ground meat, thinking we could eat it for supper, it's gone by the time I come home from work. That's why I can't shop for him in advance when I plan to go to your place after work.

Couldn't you tell him the ground meat is for supper and he'll have to eat something else when he comes home from school? I ask.

No, Jan says, he doesn't get it.

But he's twenty years old, I say. Surely it must be possible for the two of you to figure it out.

Jan sighs.

Couldn't you just have a lot of rye bread and cold cuts in the fridge for him to eat? I carry on.

I know I should stop now.

He doesn't care for that, Jan says. He prefers a hot meal after school. And if there's ground meat in the fridge, it disappears just like that.

Maybe it's also because he doesn't eat breakfast, I say, and doesn't bring a packed lunch to school.

Jan takes a deep breath.

Yes, he says. But what can I do about it? I can't get him out of bed in time for him to do it.

Couldn't you have packed a lunch for him then?

But he's twenty years old! Jan says.

I just don't understand why people can't arrange such things, I say, and grind my teeth.

Neither do I understand how there would be any room for me at Jan's row house in Lyngby. He has lived there for fifteen years with Oliver and his ex-wife. The house, located by an arterial road, is next door to his mother's row house, where he lived while growing up.

There's stuff everywhere. All the closets are already full. The ex-wife's army-green walls in the hallway. Her things in the closets. I try to clear them out and make room for my own things.

Does this thing belong to Emma? I say.

I'm standing on a ladder with my head and shoulders inside a closet.

This thing, I repeat, and from the back of the closet I pull out a felted triangle appliquéd with flowers.

What is this exactly? I ask, and extract myself from the closet.

Jan looks at it. He makes a face.

I flip the felted triangle over.

It's not particularly beautiful, I say. Is it a hat?

No, he says. It's a tea cosy.

Ah, I say, that makes more sense.

Some of Emma's girlfriends gave it to her when we got married, he says.

Hmm, I say, and throw it on the pile of stuff that's going to be tossed out.

Why are you putting it there? he says.

Isn't it going out? I say.

No, he says, and picks it up.

What then? I say. Are we supposed to use it as a tea cosy?

I'll ask Emma if she wants it, he says, putting it in the steadily growing pile of her things.

Don't you think she left it behind because she didn't want to keep it? I say.

One never knows, he says, and stares at it.

I just mean, if she had missed it, wouldn't she have asked for it by now? After all, she moved out two years ago.

I'll ask her, he says.

Hmm, I say, and squeeze my head and shoulders inside the closet again.

Two days later Emma arrives to look at the pile. She is wearing high-heeled sandals and a top with thin spaghetti straps. Jan stares closely at her arms and shoulders. The fact that she notices it is almost worse. She has lovely thin arms. I don't. He didn't tell me she was coming. Had I known, I would have dolled myself up. Instead I'm barefoot, wearing overalls. She sorts through the pile.

There's nothing here I want, she says.

Not even this? It's so cute, I say, bending down and pulling out the tea cosy.

She looks at me. And then she says:

No, not that either. You're welcome to it.

I attempt a smile but am aware of my mouth distorting, all dignity has given way and settled like ugly skin folds around it.

Emma looks at my lips and turns around.

Bye-bye, she says, and walks down the garden path.

Jan follows her. To say hi to her dog in the car.

I close the door behind them and stare at the tea cosy that hangs limp from my right hand.

Fuck, I whisper. You're such a fucking idiot, Karen.

I go into the kitchen to see if I can get a glimpse of them from the window. I can't. Then I run upstairs to the bathroom. I can't see them from there either. A long time passes before he returns.

I'm standing in the middle of the living room when he returns.

He looks at me. His pupils are very small.

Inner City of Copenhagen and Lyngby, Greater Copenhagen Area
August 2015

In addition to clearing out closets and repainting Emma's army-green walls, as well as the rest of the house, I translate. Once in a while I go to Paludan's Book Café in Fiolstræde and work there. I'm busy, and the novel I'm translating now will get a lot of attention. But suddenly I'm no longer certain how to convert meaning and rhythm and tone from one language to another. Moreover, gone is my feeling for what things are called, or how sentences are built. Or where commas are needed. I scoop up a bunch of words and try to arrange them in a reasonable sequence, but it turns out more or less random.

My writing is not going well either. I've been asked to write a literary essay about Lisbon. But I get scared when I sit down to write. I can't figure out what I'm afraid of. I am blocked.

Ida is over at the law faculty on Studiestræde working on her post-doc. We often meet up during our lunch break. Today we're at the faculty's rooftop, each with a paper plate full of salad. It's sunny, but up here it's quite windy. A piece of iceberg lettuce flies off Ida's plate and lands in her lap.

There's lettuce in your lap, Ida, I say.

Oh, she says calmly, and bends her head, looking down.

She picks it up and tries to wipe the dressing off her skirt with the edge of her hand, after which she struggles to lick the dressing off while balancing the paper plate in the strong wind.

Then she looks up at me.

Are you okay, Karen?

Yes, sure, I say, and look at her, my eyes wide.

She nods slowly and scrapes up the bits of tomato and red onion with her fork.

Why? I say.

Ida lets go of the fork.

You just seem a bit distant, she says.

Distant? I say.

Yes, distant, she says. As if you're not altogether present.

I'm probably just a little stressed, I say, looking at her.

I often wake up with a start during the night and then begin reeling off all the things I have to get done, I say.

What is it you have to get done? she says.

I take a deep breath. Then I begin. I speak quickly:

I have to make room for my things in the closets, and I have to paint. And I would really like to clean up the garden. Everything has grown into a tangled mess, and no light is coming in because the hedges have grown into trees. The narrow ones that compete for space. The place is dark and crowded. Both inside and outside. Sometimes it's hard to breathe, I say.

Ida looks at me.

And I'm also busy with the translations, I'm always behind, I say.

But I don't tell her that I have this sensation of a membrane stretched across the top part of my skull and that I'm crawling on it, frantically, not able to stand up, there isn't enough room, and when I attempt to do it anyway, I scrape my back against the inside of my skull.

Neither do I tell her that while I run desperately around the garden clearing away the ivy from the windows and removing fallen branches in an attempt to create some space around myself, the voices in the tiny space at the top of my skull natter away in a never-ending discussion about whether I'm a bad woman who, in the larger area below the membrane, houses a wild beast that I'm hell-bent on suppressing, or whether the beast down there, in actual fact, has something sensible to tell me. About my longing to look into a pair of eyes and having long conversations, my need for space, wishing I didn't have to remind myself not to be disruptive with my presence when Jan comes home from work, about my longing for complete openness that lets the light in, about whether this longing is valid. Whether it's reasonable or unreasonable to listen to it.

I make up my mind that it's unreasonable. Admittedly I behave like a neurotic when running around like that, I know it, and I can see it in Jan's eyes. I'll have to learn to rein in the wild beast that lives below the distended membrane. I know very well how respectable people behave. They are self-controlled, tolerant, and understanding.

But when Oliver comes home from school and flings himself down on the couch and turns on the TV right next to the table where I'm working, irritation surges inside me again. We have only one living room. And Jan and I have agreed that Oliver should always feel welcome there as a matter of course. It is hard enough for him to get used to me living there, running around and tidying up. It will not do if I take over the living room as well and make it my study. I move into the bedroom and sit on the bed with my Mac. At other times I keep working in the living room. I smile and say he can keep watching TV. But I don't understand why he doesn't have other things to do. See friends. Play some sports or go to the library. Do homework. Is there nothing else for him to do than just lie on the couch watching TV? I try smiling at him again. I feel I'm going about this the wrong way, the smile is a grimace, and he's looking away.

But in a more or less acceptable manner, I manage to introduce a rule that when we eat—Jan, Oliver, and I—we talk to each other and don't sit in front of the TV with our plates of pasta and meat sauce balanced on our laps. I ask Oliver and Jan about things, inquire about this and that, try desperately to keep the conversation going. I'm thinking that surely they'll soon find out how wonderful it is to talk to one another when you eat together. It doesn't occur to me that I'm the only one who craves it.

I don't need attention all that much, Jan says.

And Oliver tells me it's difficult for him to make eye contact with people.

How does that feel? I ask him.

Exhausting, he says, looking down and off to the side.

Nonetheless we slowly begin finding each other, Oliver and I. I prepare extra-large portions for dinner and put them in plastic containers he can bring with him to school, and we work out a system in the fridge so it's easy to remember what may be consumed freely and what should be left alone. And one day, finally, he comes downstairs to the living room holding my concealer in his hand. He stands a few metres from me, looking a bit shy.

Then he says:

Can you help me?

I look up from the Mac.

Yes, I say.

I have a pimple, he says, and looks away while holding out the concealer.

I can certainly help you with that, I say, pushing a chair in front of my own.

He sits down and points at a red spot on his chin.

I unscrew the lid of the concealer and put a small amount on my fingertip. While I dab it on the spot, he looks up sideways and to the right, and I'm overcome by a feeling of tenderness for him and curse myself for having shown my irritation.

I wonder if I'm like my father, I think.

Sortedam Dossering
Nørrebro Neighbourhood in Copenhagen
24 October 2015

After one week I'm discharged and transferred to the Psychotherapy Outpatient Clinic at the Ballerup Psychiatric Centre, where I'll see both the hippie psychiatrist and a young psychotherapist called Eskild.

Selma and I have moved in with Anne and Mikkel temporarily. We live on two mattresses in their living room.

May I have a closet, Mom? she asks again. Or some shelves?

Yes, of course, I say. Obviously you need some shelves for your things.

But although she does get her two shelves, she feels anguished. Homeless, causing inconvenience on a mattress in somebody else's living room. She moves in with her boyfriend.

I have fucking failed to live up to the most important job ever: I've been unable to take care of my child.

I stopped eating a long time ago. Sometimes Mikkel looks at me and says:

Eat this, Karen. Now!

He hands me something or other.

I take it, not knowing what it is. It swells up in my mouth, turns over like a big ball of regurgitated owl pellet behind my teeth that still grow forward and out of my mouth. When I touch the back of my front teeth with my tongue, I can feel that they are horizontal. I try swallowing the ball in the front of my mouth. I don't know how to move it further back. It's supposed to move away from my horizontal teeth, pass across my tongue, and hit the hole that leads into my body. I have no problem understanding that. I poke my finger inside and try nudging the ball in the right direction.

Sønder Vilstrup, Jutland
The 1970s

What I should be:
  A boy
  Alternatively a tomboy
  A wild child
  Strong and graceful, standing up straight
  Cheeky
  The best student in all school subjects except for mathematics
  Very good at athletics, especially sprint and long jump, disciplines that demand strength and bursts of energy
  Very good at acrobatic jumps and cartwheels
  Good at rope climbing and lateral arm swings
  Exceptionally good at drawing, skating, and skiing
  Good at handling a knife and knowing the difference between north and south by observing the amount of lichen on tree trunks
  Good at singing and playing music
  Curious
  Fearless, daring to hang upside down in tall trees.

What I shouldn't be or do:
  Lazy, idle, and lethargic
  Feel anxiety

Dream of being a girl and doing girlish things such as combing my hair or wearing dresses.

But I do have certain shameful fantasies. For example, wearing barrettes and my mother's high-heeled shoes. Those kinds of things happen in the same secret places where masturbation later takes place. In the hideout under the red currant bushes. In my room while I listen for sounds coming from the stairs. Or when I walk into a dense thicket, blushing, and say I've lost something two metres further into the thicket, just so no one will see my mother's shoes.

Props Coffee Shop
Blågårdsgade
Nørrebro Neighbourhood in Copenhagen
16 October 2015

You're drinking that beer very quickly, Jan says.
   Yes, I say, and smile. That's because I enjoy being here.
   I feel like letting loose.
   His jaw is tensing up.
   I step over and stand in front of him, look into his face with a broad smile, teeth showing.
   I love it here, talking to people who do the same thing as I do and who are interested in the same things as me, I say, gesticulating wildly. It's not often we meet because we work isolated from each other.
   I get it, he says. But perhaps you could hold back on the beer?
   Why should I do that? I say. I'm feeling great.
   We've been to a poetry reading, and now we're at Props with a bunch of the poets. My friend who is bipolar is here too. His large body can hold an enormous amount of alcohol, but the only thing that happens is his energy level spirals in tandem with his alcohol intake. He speaks louder, his hands and arms take up more space. I'm fascinated by his not giving a damn, and obviously I want to turn the energy level up as well.
   But I'm here with Jan. And for Jan there's no letting loose.

He looks at his watch. We have a train to catch. We have to leave this place, the city, we're going out to the suburbs.

I stagger onto the train. The wild beast below the membrane in my skull is wriggling. I'm drunk, I don't care, I feel like swinging along with the beast when it wags its tail.

Why do you insist on living right next door to your mother? I say. The place where you have always lived. Don't you crave adventure? Getting out of your comfort zone just a little bit?

He doesn't answer. I lean back.

I hate arterial roads, I say to no one in particular. The street lights are way up and cast this white light over everything.

He sighs.

Don't you ever feel like stepping out of your house and seeing people who are unconventional and odd and not just nice ladies from Lyngby?

He turns toward me.

No! he says.

The next morning I wake up with a start. I'm covered in shame. Fearing the wild beast—and all the things I and the beast destroy when banding together.

I apologize with my eyes full of despair.

I want to be a small animal that curls up under the hedge, I say, sitting down on the kitchen stool.

Jan smiles. He's preparing dinner. His family is coming.

I'm not sure I have enough strength to get through this evening, I say. I'm tired, so very tired.

I'm sorry about that, he says. But it will mean a lot to me if you're present tonight.

I nod. Look down at the palms of my hands.

Okay, I say, I understand.

It would be hard for him to explain that Karen is lying outside under the hedge. I realize that.

Is Oliver finished in the bathroom? I say.

Yes, he says while collecting the potato peels in the sink.

I press my hands against the stool and push myself up.

Then I'll take a shower, I say.

He nods.

And make an attempt at being civilized, I add on my way out the door.

I'm a made-up hostess when the guests arrive: Jan's mother, his brother and his wife, and their grown-up daughters.

The doorbell rings, and I open the door.

The first in line is Laila. She's holding a bouquet of pink roses and hands it to me. I smile and smell them, although I know very well that the roses we buy in the stores don't have any fragrance. Nevertheless, I say:

Ah, they smell so nice! Thank you, Laila, please come in.

I make room so they can step into the hallway. We kiss on the cheek, Laila and I. And my brother-in-law, Christian, looks me in the eye. I like looking into his eyes, they always seem warm. He puts his arms around my shoulders and pulls me toward him.

Welcome, I say, nice to see you!

Thank you, it's nice to see you too, Karen, he says.

The daughters, Julie and Simone, are already inside, they are chatting away, laughing, I can't make out what they are saying. Oliver is standing in the background looking ill at ease. He takes a step toward the cousins but backs off quickly. The last one is Aase. She looks down at the threshold before carefully stepping over it. I hug her and give her a kiss on the cheek, she gives me one in return.

It smells delicious in here, she says.

I turn toward Jan.

Thanks to Jan, I say, he cooked all the food.

Now, please, come in, I say, and have a glass of wine. It's very cold tonight, isn't it?

That's for sure, Laila says, rubbing her hands together.

Jan goes back into the kitchen to tend to the food. I pour the wine and pass the glasses around. The muscles around my left eye are trembling. I don't know if it's noticeable, but I rub the area repeatedly to make the muscles relax.

Would you like some wine too, Oliver? I ask, looking up at him, holding an empty wineglass in my hand.

He hesitates.

There's cola as well, I say. Would you rather have that?

He takes a step toward me with a sense of purpose.

I would like wine, he says.

I pour him a glass.

Thank you, he says, taking the glass.

And you, honey? I say, and look at Jan, who has returned from the kitchen and now stands quietly beside me.

Yes, please, he says.

Christian, Laila, Julie, and Simone are talking loudly. It is not clear to the rest of us what they are talking about. But from what I can glean from the conversation, Julie's boyfriend has managed to borrow a trailer from an old schoolmate.

The food is ready now, Jan whispers to me.

Shouldn't we serve it then? I say.

Yes, he says.

We go into the kitchen. Oliver follows, and the three of us carry in bowls and platters.

Please, be seated, Jan says.

It looks great, Jan, Christian says, eyeing the food approvingly. Your favourite dish.

He laughs.

Jan always makes osso buco, Christian says, addressing me.

Jan doesn't say anything.

It looks delicious, Laila says.

While the bowls are being passed around, I ask Laila, who's sitting at the other end of the table, how it feels being back at work. After a long sick leave, she's now back working for home care services. It feels good, obviously she's tired a lot, but it's okay. And it's nice being active again.

That's good to hear, I say.

I keep an eye on the wineglasses. I'm a good hostess. I pass a bottle to Oliver, who sits across from me.

Can you reach over and pour some for Christian? I ask.

Yes, he says, and takes the bottle from me. He holds on to it for a bit.

Do you want more wine, Christian? he says.

Christian looks at Oliver.

Yes, please, fill it up. He turns toward Simone, who's in the middle of some story. About the nursing program, I think.

I have a feeling that I can't hear very well tonight. It's quiet at my end of the table, at the other end the noise level is rising, they are laughing, talking, faster and faster. No one is asking questions. Not to anyone at our end, but not to each other either as far as I can hear, they speak all at once, my in-laws. I try to figure out what they are talking about. Their sentences are not forming interlacing threads. More like balls on the loose. In a pinball machine. I can't follow them any longer. I can't find any mounds to jump on in the intersection of these distinct mathematical sets, I can't find any common ground.

I clear my throat as if I'm going to say something.

Laila glances at me. But since I don't say anything, she turns toward Julie again.

I clear my throat again, and I say in a loud, authoritative voice: I'm writing an article right now.

I don't know why I'm saying it. Everyone turns and looks at me. The room falls silent. My voice is a lid, causing the word balls that are ricocheting back and forth across the table to crash.

About Lisbon, I continue.

They look at me.

And Pessoa, I say. A Portuguese writer who did an exceptional thing in that he split up the author's self into many heteronyms.

I speak articulately and am careful to face each one in turn around the table. Like when I give lectures.

Heteronyms are a type of authorial identities, each with its own biography, philosophical position, and poetic voice, I continue. And when they had broken out of Pessoa, in a manner of speaking, they lived as fictive characters in polemics with each other and with Pessoa, and each with their own literary work. You could say they are shells where each acts like a complete, filled-out identity, but together they are contained within this singular, divided self.

All faces are turned toward me, nobody is saying anything. The words dribble out of my mouth. Then my head drops toward my shoulder and I close my eyes. I stop talking. I don't know if they continue with their chatting, I can't hear anything.

I push my chair back carefully, get up from the table, and sneak out.

I go upstairs. I think I'm on my way to the bathroom, but in fact I'm walking into the room right above the dining room. There's a stack of books on the windowsill. I grab them. I walk to the centre of the room, raise the stack high above my head, and slam it onto the floor. The crash is loud. I look around me. There are two bookcases leaning against the wall. I knock them over and they fly across the wooden floor. I don't know why I'm doing it. Then I see Jan out in the hallway. The door is open. I'm holding something in my hand, it's the door handle, I slam the door in his face. It flies open, I slam it, it flies open, and I whack it, bang it, again and again, the taut membrane at the top of my skull bursts, it feels euphoric, wonderful, liberating, I see images of cascading water that bursts dams and gushes with wild and uncontrollable force.

I let go of the door handle and walk past Jan and down the stairs.

Oliver is on his way up the stairs. He looks frightened. Presses himself up against the wall. I walk down through the middle of the stairs. When we pass each other, I snarl at him.

Don't you have any dreams? I hiss. Is your life nothing else but lying on the couch watching TV? Don't you want to use it for anything?

He doesn't answer, he's already past me, shuts himself inside his room.

I go downstairs to the entrance hall. There's not a soul left. I don't know which way to go. I walk to the kitchen, quickly, stand in front of the magnetic strip on the wall, and look at the knives. I take the longest one. Walk back to the entrance hall.

Jan is standing in front of me.

Suddenly I burst into tears.

I'm going to kill myself with this, I say.

I know there isn't any other way out now.

I hit Jan hard in the chest with my free hand. He catches hold of me, turns me around, lifts me off the floor, my back against his stomach. I hang from his arms, I try to wriggle myself free and jerk my head fiercely in all directions.

Oliver comes running down the stairs again. He shouts:
KAREN, YOU'RE FUCKING INSANE!

It hurts so much, so incredibly much.

Jan shouts at him while keeping a tight hold on me:
GET AWAY FROM HERE! GET SOMEWHERE SAFE!

Oliver is outside. The door slams shut behind him. My body goes limp. The knife falls to the floor, and I hang heavily in Jan's arms.

I'm ill, I whisper.

69

I try meeting his gaze.

Jan lets me go.

I have to be committed, I say. Phone them now. Psychiatric emergency.

He walks over to the phone. Dials. I can't hear what he's saying, I go into the bedroom and start stuffing clothes into a gym bag. I'm empty. I'm hollow. The human being in me is gone.

PART
TWO

Sønder Vilstrup, Jutland
The 1970s

There's a smell of old hay and motor oil in the barn. We have two Volvo 544s and a parked, beat-up Massey Ferguson without a cab. I'm in the process of braiding some of the bailing twine that's fastened on a rusty ring and hanging from one of the heavy support beams in the centre of the barn. My mother comes in to collect something. I look up.

What are we having for supper? I ask.

Pancakes, she replies.

I let go of the twine, run over to her, throw my arms around her belly, and say:

I love you.

She lets me hold on to her. Her arms hang down by her sides. Then she says:

You're only saying that because we're having pancakes.

I'm not completely certain it was my reason for saying it, but I'm ashamed and feel the heat rising on my face. I let go of her and walk back to the bailing twine. I can hear her footsteps on the gravel in the barnyard and the door to the scullery closing behind her.

We play a lot in the barn, Niels and I. You can climb way up on the bales of hay that are stacked to the top beams, and from there you can jump down onto the loose hay, many, many metres below, and when you're suspended in the air in the semi-dark barn and hear the rain drumming on the metal roof, the thrill gives you crazy butterflies. Niels is always more afraid than me. It's because he's so little. He's very thin and has white-blond hair and round, sun-tanned cheeks.

My dad doesn't show much affection for him.

Perhaps because he isn't brave. Or because he can't draw or play music like I can, for instance. Or else because he isn't Jens.

Jens had brown hair like me. Niels and Anne have the same white-blond hair. Perhaps we're actually divided into groups according to hair colour.

Niels was born shortly after Jens died.

You better hurry up and have another child, the doctors said to my mother and father.

My mother weighs less after having given birth to him than before she became pregnant. She's terribly thin, wasted, and Niels is also terribly thin and wasted when he first enters the world. They have worn each other out. He continues being thin for a very long time, and she does as well. My father talks about Kierkegaard and anxiety and pain, about facing our losses and the suffering that life necessarily has in store for us, but my mother is a sled without a lead dog—tied to a pack of feelings that pull her to and fro. And during the first many years, she's so unhappy that barely anything works for her. And the idea of replacing the dead child with Niels doesn't work for her at all.

But after a while it does. Or perhaps something else happens. In any case, she ends up loving him. She embraces him like you would a small, scruffy-looking chick, and she protects him from our father.

Niels doesn't make as much of an effort trying to be the dead child as I do. He takes off and goes elsewhere. To see Andreas, for instance, who owns the neighbouring farm. I have a feeling that Niels, or whoever decided on the alliances, is the wiser for allying himself with my mother as opposed to me, who has allied myself with my father.

Even though my mother is usually sad or testy or has a headache, you still feel more at ease with her than with my father. When she's happy, she'll push my father with all his jazz and classical music away from the grand piano and sit down, one foot on the pedal and the other far out to the side. Her face is radiant with joy, she looks like a mischievous girl to me, and I spin around next to her. And then she'll play rock 'n' roll! With her fingers stretched out while hammering up and down the keyboard.

On Saturday nights she's also happy. As we all are. My father and Anne soften sheets of gelatine. They are making lemon soufflé, and I slide out to them in the kitchen in my stocking feet, or I lie down on my back under the table in the dining room and push myself around in a circle with my feet until I lose interest and run back to them in the kitchen again.

I know that nothing bad will happen.

Psychotherapy Outpatient Clinic
Ballerup, Greater Copenhagen Area
November 2015

I put on makeup. I can't feel it, but when I look in the mirror I see that I have an outer covering, a shell. That's what I'm painting.

The S-train takes me from Nørreport to Malmparken Station. The windswept platform is elevated above the main road. Out here the streets have names related to industry, energy, mining, and speed. I go down the stairs and take shelter under the bridge. The wind is howling. The bus leaves every twenty minutes, I never manage to catch it, although I always check the schedule. Bus 350 doesn't run according to the timetable. That's what I tell the driver. Something has to be done about it, I say to him. He looks at me but doesn't answer. I'm one of those who gets off at the Ballerup Psychiatric Centre.

The hippie psychiatrist asks me to sit down at a round table.

We sit there for an hour and a half, I'm tired, feeling cold as usual. I stare at her through my hunger holes.

How many times have you moved in your life? she asks.

I think about it, count on my fingers, give her a pleading look, reel off the times I can remember.

She cuts me off.

That will do, she says, and writes something down.

Please, I say, my siblings misunderstood my boyfriend. I was threatening myself, not Jan, with the knife. Can you change that in the record?

I can't change it, but I can add the information.

Thank you, I say.

She writes on her notepad.

The worst part is that I cannot write, I say, looking up at her.

She pushes the notepad off to the side and looks at me.

Then she says:

Karen?

I look up.

Yes?

Your illness could've been a lot more serious than it is. What prevented it from happening is your intelligence. Because of that it was possible for you to establish some sophisticated coping strategies and defence mechanisms.

She leans still closer to me.

They've been very useful to you and have helped you. But you don't need them any longer. Now it's time to unlearn them.

My eyes cling to hers.

Your therapist, Eskild, will help you with all that, she says. You're also in a very fortunate position in that you're therapy-ready. You're not opposed to therapy, which is something we often see.

No, I'm not opposed, I say. I'm like "Bring it on."

I gesture with my hands as if I'm shovelling something into my mouth.

That's good, she says.

I *want* to get well! I say with a determined look.

You will, and you'll also be able to write again.

The last part I'm not sure I dare to believe.

Nørreport Neighbourhood in Copenhagen
November 2015

It's cold now. I only have a short blazer and a scarf. The rest of my things are still at Jan's place in Lyngby.

The reason I've written and asked him about my coat is not so much about getting it back.

I haven't seen him since he took me to the ER at the Psychiatric Centre, but we have spoken on the phone a couple of times.

He's standing in front of the 7-Eleven. I cross the square. He's looking at me while I walk toward him.

I stop in front of him.

Hi, I say cautiously.

Hi, he says.

There's a sparkle in his eyes.

You have braided your hair the fancy way, he says fondly.

Yes, I say.

We look at each other. Not saying anything.

Then he bends down and digs into his bag.

Here, he says. Your coat.

Sønder Vilstrup, Jutland
The 1970s

We have a long dining table with a bench along one side, a chair at one end, and two chairs opposite the bench. Niels and I, who have the poorest conversation skills, regularly occupy the furthermost seats, Niels at the end of the bench by the wall and I across from him on the chair.

We know very well why these seats are ours. Here too Niels uses his quick getaway strategy. When we've finished eating, he slides under the table, crawls on all fours, and surfaces on the other side. He sits down with his Lego blocks or runs over to Andreas's place or lies down on his stomach on the floor with his atlas, which is almost bigger than him. He knows the names of all the rivers in the world. And the cities and the countries and the mountains, and he knows how many people live in each city.

I remain in my seat and listen. I'm like our black Labrador, Linka, my father says, I like the family being gathered and that we talk. My father thinks Anne is more clever than us, and I'm sad to not be as clever, for if I was maybe I could move closer toward the end of the table and engage more with the rest of the family and even be asked questions. It takes several years before it hits me that the reason Anne is so clever is because she's four years older than me and seven years older than Niels.

Psychotherapy Outpatient Clinic
Ballerup, Greater Copenhagen Area
November 2015

I attend cognitive behavioural therapy sessions with Eskild twice a week. He's my care worker, and I'm allowed to call him directly on his mobile.

Eskild wants me to participate in group therapy at the outpatient clinic. He says I'll probably find that I'm better adjusted and treatment-ready than the others. That's why I'm worried.

But I do as they say and go there on a Thursday morning. We sit around a large oval conference table. We're fifteen people of which two are new. Me and a young man with a beard and a large overweight body. He's wearing a nice light-blue shirt buttoned up to the top. He's standing outside the door as if he needs to assess the situation before entering.

At last he crosses the threshold. He holds a plastic cup of water in his hand. His hand is shaking violently, and the water spills over with each step he takes. Slowly, step by step, he enters the room. He has picked out a seat for himself next to the therapists on the far side of the table, opposite me, getting there is taking a long time. He has to negotiate large obstacles to reach his destination, what with his trembling hand and the water that keeps slopping over. I don't know if the floor slopes and threatens to throw him off, or if there are mocking voices in his head tearing him to pieces.

Finally he gets there. He looks relieved. But it doesn't last long. Because now the therapists ask us to introduce ourselves, seeing that the two of us are new, and he's being asked to go first. Most likely he had thought that the seat beside the therapists would be the safest.

He opens his mouth, his lips trembling, but nothing comes out. Sweat runs down his brow and face. He shakes more and more, now his entire body is shaking. Tension can be felt around the table. The therapists try getting him to stand up, they want him out of the room. His hands are cramped in an awkward contorted position. Slowly, slowly do they manage to usher him out of there, still shaking, and just when they are out the door his ankles buckle under him and he lands with his insteps dragging on the floor.

Clearly he cannot keep his balance in that position, so it's up to the women to support his large, limp body and twisted feet. The door closes.

The woman with a full-sleeve tattoo sitting beside me pounds the table frantically with her hand.

Fuck! she says. What the hell is *he* doing here?

For fuck's sake, a woman across from her says. Surely he has as much right to be here as you do.

I don't say anything. Just sit motionless, keeping my head down.

The leg belonging to the man next to me is bouncing up and down.

Soon the therapists return.

It was an anxiety attack, they say.

I had no idea anxiety could result in feet like that.

The others are still feeling restless, it's as if their nerves are bleeding excess dye that taints the others. One of the women shoves her chair back and says:

I can't stand it here today, dammit! There are too many new ones.

I happen to be one of those she's referring to.

Several of the others say that it's true, new people create too much commotion.

The therapists say that nothing can be done about it.

The woman gets up. The chair falls over behind her.

I can't fucking stand it any longer. It drives me insane being here, she shouts.

My body feels narrow and rigid, incapable of moving.

The therapists ask us to describe how our mood has been during the past week on a scale from 1 to 100, where the interval between 40 and 50 means normal, and 1 is suffering of the most severe kind. Most of the estimates are around 20 to 30, but mine is down at 10.

I can't recognize my own voice. It's dark, strained.

I'm crying, can't hold back. Silence has descended over the table now, the rest of them are observing me closely.

I tell them I'm missing my boyfriend, whom I loved, and who left me after I was committed.

You just don't do that kind of thing, one of them says.

It was my fault, I say.

How? a young man says, leaning back in his chair, his hands buried deep in the pockets of his hoodie.

I look at him.

I became ill and had a psychotic episode and did some awful things. I can't remember anything from the evening when it happened. But I've been told that I slammed a stack of books onto the floor and hit him and grabbed a knife because I wanted to take my own life.

I take a breath, and then I say:

I've wrecked everything.

But you were ill. It wasn't something that you had decided to do, he says.

A woman says:

If he walked out on you while you were fucking sick and committed, then he isn't worth a fucking damn.

I dislike the way she talks about Jan. Nevertheless I feel that her straightforward, unambiguous support is taking effect. We practise solidarity here.

I continue:

Although I was ill, I've actually been working the whole time as a translator, I say. But perhaps it was all too much.

You're totally awesome! the young guy says.

I send him a smile. A warm sensation unfolds in my body that usually feels cold, now that it has become so thin.

Sønder Vilstrup, Jutland
The 1970s

My father is the one who likes me. But I usually feel ill at ease in his company. So it's not nice when my mother has a migraine and goes to bed and is gone all day and night.

My father's papers and books are scattered all over the dining table. The light doesn't get turned on. Niels is sitting on the floor tucked into the corner with his atlas. Anne isn't here. Unwittingly I've been biting my nails to the point where my fingers have begun to bleed. It's ugly. I wrap some tape around my fingertips and paint them red so it looks as if I have long red nails.

When Anne comes home, we go upstairs to our mother. She starts crying and says that she isn't a good mother.

Oh, but you are! we say.

Sortedam Dossering
Nørrebro Neighbourhood in Copenhagen
November 2015

Anne and I are sitting on the couch in her living room, I'm cold. My mattress and my duvet and pillow lie in the corner below the window. My suitcase is on top. I'm taking up so much space. I constantly try reorganizing my things and tidying up. Gathering everything I have and placing it on the mattress. Stuffing it into the suitcase so the mattress doesn't get cluttered up.

I'm a difficult guest. I don't contribute to their conversations. I can't hear what people are saying.

We give up having a conversation. Anne reaches for the newspaper *Information* on the coffee table, I open my Mac. There's an email in my inbox. From the hippie psychiatrist. She confirms an appointment, and then she writes:

By the way, the test you have completed for me clearly demonstrates that you have a sufficient number of character traits to meet the diagnostic criteria that correspond to an emotionally unstable personality disorder of the borderline type, which I have been thinking as well, following our conversations.

My pulse is racing, in a split second I've become inflamed with anxiety. I get up. Start pacing.

Oh no! Oh no! I say.

Anne looks alarmed.

What's happening? she says.

Read the email! I say despairingly.

Anne puts the Mac on her lap and reads. Then she says:

Come here, sit down.

She points to the spot next to her on the couch.

She's aware that this is the diagnosis I fear the most. It's without hope. It's a life sentence. It's hideous.

My hands are shaking. Anne sits hunched up beside me. I jump up, go over to the suitcase on the mattress. I unzip it and look for the small green book issued by World Heath Organization, the ICD-10 *Classification of Mental and Behavioural Disorders: Diagnostic Criteria for Research*. This is the one that's used in psychiatry. I tend to cart around a mountain of psychiatric literature. I leaf through it. Point at the diagnostic criteria for borderline personality disorder. Anne tries to follow along. Then I close the book and start googling frantically on the internet. I read things out loud to Anne. Up until now she has been unwilling to hear about the various diagnoses. But now she has to. I read, quickly, tripping over the words:

Personality disorder (PD) is characterized by personality traits that:
- *are persistent, deep-seated, and rigid patterns of feeling, of thinking, and of relating to people*
- *deviate markedly from the expectations of the individual's culture*
- *are stable over time*
- *have an onset in adolescence or early adulthood*

- are often associated with increased subjective discomfort and impaired social adaptability

Emotionally unstable personality disorder (borderline personality disorder) is a serious mental disorder characterized by
- *an enduring unstable pattern regarding emotional adjustment, impulsivity, interpersonal relationships, and self-image*
Personality disorders are heterogeneous in their clinical features and etiology

Anne's face has gone blank.

That's terrible! I say.

Anne doesn't say anything.

I get up again, dig out a couple more books. Point at pages and lines.

We're also manipulative, I say. It's mentioned in several places.

I give her a desperate look.

We? Anne says.

We're about the most disgusting people on this earth. Perhaps except for those with anti-social personality disorder, the psychopaths, I say.

Anne holds up her hands.

Excuse me, Karen, she says.

She sounds almost angry.

What? I say. I'm standing in front of her with a stack of books in my arms.

Actually, to be honest, I don't want to listen to this anymore, she says.

I stare at her, shocked.

I simply can't take it in, she says. I want to relate to *you*. I'm not sure I recognize you in all that other stuff.

I am angry with her. I'm weighed down by this pervasive, lifelong distrust of my humanity. BPD can't be treated, I've read this in several places. I've also read that we're the patients that care workers at psychiatric hospitals fear the most because we're manipulative and play the staff one against the other. We're the worst of all human beings.

Anne gets up.

I'll make us some tea, she says.

I pace the room. I've been looking forward to a diagnosis, to being granted an identity. But the diagnosis she has given me is for people without an identity. Honest to God, how is this of any use to me? And, as a matter of fact, I could easily have an identity, but I'm unable to maintain it for any length of time. I'm a serial user of identites.

Tension, tension, tension is building up in my jaw, and I don't believe that I deserve all this. I've fought my case, had hour-long conversations with psychiatrists and psychologists, and of course I could sense how I charmed all of them, I can be quite eloquent when I want to be, even during a psychotic episode, and modest and polite, and my mouth is smiling, and I have large healthy teeth, and not a soul knows who I am, and people often pretend not to recognize me when I meet them on the street, and I pretend like-wise, once I knew many people and we greeted each other, and I've made sure to show my gratitude to the psychiatrists, I'm a good patient, I'm nice, I'm interesting, I'm intelligent, I have a gift for language, and they think it's marvellous that I've written novels, and I've been acutely aware of what I've said and not said, because everything I say and don't say, and do and don't do, is being weighed and measured, and I stand on a stool, naked, in front of them and turn around and lean my head back and open my mouth so they can look inside, behind my large teeth and deep down my throat.

Kate's Joint
Blågårdsgade
Nørrebro Neighbourhood in Copenhagen
November 2015

Ida has a different body than me, now that mine has become what it is.

She's sitting calmly on her chair. Doesn't fidget. Doesn't shift her legs about. Ida remains in the same position for a long time. Her eyes are focused on me.

Ida wants me to eat something.

She takes me down to Blågårdsgade. She thinks we should look for some food. We walk side by side. I don't know if I'm talking. I think it's going well, that I'm moving along in an appropriate manner. I easily make my way around the people and the tables outside Props and Harbo Bar. But something is not as it should be, for suddenly, out of the blue, she stops and faces me. Maybe I'm talking too much.

Karen, she says.

The expression on her face worries me.

Come over here, she says, and opens her arms.

I step into her arms.

She holds me tight for a long time. I'm aware that she wants me to stand still without saying anything, her arms around me.

I do as she wants but don't know why we're embracing.

Then she lets go of me and takes my hand.

Let's go in here, she says.

I nod.

We go into Kate's Joint, and Ida tells me where to sit.

Yes, I say, sitting down at the table she's pointing at.

Ida doesn't give me the menu. Neither does she ask me what I would like to have. She walks directly over to the counter and talks to a waiter. Then she returns and sits down beside me on the bench. I can feel her body on my right. I can feel that our arms and thighs are touching. I'm not sure if I'm talking, but my eyes are fixed on her the whole time. Her face is turned toward me.

Food is brought to our table.

Ida pushes the plate in my direction and puts down a fork close to my left hand.

I'm probably talking. Ida looks me in the eye. But then she looks down at my hand. She nods toward it.

Now pick up your fork, Karen, she says.

I look at it, grab it. It's warm. Maybe it's come straight from the dishwasher.

The food looks wonderful, she says.

Yes, I say, looking at her.

There's rice, she says, and curried lamb. It looks delicious.

I look down at the food. I sense that Ida really wants me to eat.

I stick the fork into the food. Then I take the knife in the other hand and push something onto the fork.

It looks really delicious, she says.

I lift the fork to my mouth and shove it in. It's a strange sensation. As if the food and the fork are penetrating me. I pull out the fork and leave the food inside. It feels warm. It feels unfamiliar. But I'm able to swallow it.

Ida is eating. Ida eats a lot, and it surprises me how fast she can do it. Within a short time, only half the meal is left on her plate.

It tastes great, she says.

I understand now that it means I'm supposed to grab my fork again and use it to shove more food into my mouth. Which I do. Three more times.

Enough. I should be allowed to put my fork down now. I put my fork down, and Ida lets me. Her plate is empty now.

I place the palms of my hands against the table and push myself up. I feel dizzy when I stand.

Look! I say, and point at my jeans and my stomach and thighs.

Ida looks at my stomach and thighs.

I've lost weight, I say, smiling. Doesn't it look great?

Ida nods slowly.

Sure, she says.

Ida can look exceptionally sad. I sit down again, and we don't talk about it any more.

Sankt Hans Gade Passage
Nørrebro Neighbourhood in Copenhagen
November 2015

My friend Lone has found an apartment for me by Sankt Hans Torv that is available for a month. I can tell from Anne's and Mikkel's faces that me staying in their living room has started to get on their nerves. They are not saying anything, but I can tell. It's also getting to me.

It's a one-bedroom apartment in an alley behind the firehall. The young woman who lives there has put a bouquet of flowers and an enormous bowl with candies on the table. All for me. My eyes fill with tears. She hands me the keys and leaves.

The first thing I do is go to the kitchen to turn on the radio. P8 Jazz comes on. I flinch. Turn it off. Move back a step. I used to listen to P8 Jazz with Jan. I want to change to P1 Culture and Ideas. I fumble with the tuning. It's absolutely paramount that I find P1. The first day I don't succeed. But the next day I finally manage to hit the correct buttons, and there it is.

When I return to the apartment after I've been out, I go into the kitchen and turn on P1 before taking my coat off. I can't handle any kind of music, especially not jazz.

I need money.

There's no weighted blanket here, but I sit down on the couch with an ordinary duvet wrapped tightly around me and start

translating. A Norwegian novel, thank God it is Norwegian—
after all, it's easier to translate from Norwegian than from
Swedish or English—when concentration can only be sum-
moned to a tiny, thin area of my brain.

P1 is on. P1 takes away anxiety.

I have a supply of benzodiazepines, I carry them with me
everywhere. But I try to avoid them, I'm afraid of them. Benzodiazepines can turn you into an addict. Sometimes I can't
escape them. Then I swallow a tiny pill that makes my arms
tingle, and I slump against the back of the couch. It empties my
brain. Makes it feel detached.

Maybe one day I'll take my Mac and sit at one of the tall
tables by the window in Kaffeplantagen, the café on Sankt Hans
Torv. The deadline for my article on Lisbon is soon approaching.
I haven't been able to write in a long while, but right now it
seems to go rather well.

I fantasize that the article is about Jan and me and that I've
made a scene in the middle of Jardim do Príncipe Real and he
has turned on his heel and split. That I'm no longer reflected in
his gaze. That I charge around the city looking for him, including at the Pessoa museum, where I snap up identities for myself.
They hang from coat hangers in there. And as if I don't have
anything else to do, I put them on, in the beginning all goes
well, but after a while they start cutting into my armpits, there
are too many of them, and the identities of others don't necessarily fit around your arms and neck.

Finally it hits me where I might find him: at Hot Clube de
Portugal. The old jazz club on Praça da Alegria.

I walk down the unlit stairs to Hot Clube, which is located
below street level. I see him down there, leaning against the
wall with his eyes closed. There's *no* sign of another woman

sitting with him. A beer is in front of him on the table. His one hand lies relaxed beside it. His body shows no movement. I don't know anyone like him who can sit motionless, contemplating. Or being empty. Perhaps he can stop time and with it descend into a state of non-being? I can't, there's a distended membrane around my emptiness, I'm lying inside the shell of my skin. Naturally I have dolled myself up for this mission. I'm wearing a knee-length dress and black high-heeled sandals. My mouth is painted. I sit down across from him at the tables on the other side of the open floor. Cross my legs. Try to sit as composed as he is.

A trio is playing on the stage. The drummer is leaning over his drums, his ear turned toward his brushes that are working on the taut skin. I look at Jan. Place my hand on the table like him. Then he opens his eyes, his head still leaning against the wall. He looks at me. I'm a stranger.

Props Coffee Shop
Blågårdsgade
Nørrebro Neighbourhood in Copenhagen
November 2015

Jan wants to forget me. Won't talk to me. Wants to move on, as they say. I believe moving on is about forgetting the fact there once was a person in your life.

I've only one weapon against oblivion: my clothes and my furniture are still at his place.

I have requested a dress, a pair of jeans, underpants, a few tops. Surprisingly, he has agreed to deliver the clothes to me at Props and not outside, say, at Nørreport Station. I make sure to arrive before him so as to have time to check myself in front of the bathroom mirror. My hands are shaking as I apply lip gloss. It smears outside the edges. I wipe it off. With my hands grabbing the edge of the sink, I lean forward and close my eyes. Karen, Karen, Karen, you exist, I whisper.

I sit down in the back of the room at a table I think is most suitable for conversation. I wait. Check my mobile. Keep an eye on the door.

Then he shows up. All in black. He scans the room. Sees me. Walks toward me. I get up and approach him. He screws up his eyes. Looks at me, looks me over. Takes a deep breath, I notice it from his rib cage, which expands, then relaxes.

He kisses me quickly and absently on the cheek.

They have nice, freshly made ginger tea, I say.

Okay? he says.

Would you like some? I say.

Yes, it sounds good, he says.

I buy two. We sit down. I sit on the bench with my legs crossed. He sits opposite me.

We hardly say a word. Drink our tea. Look at each other a bit. Look away.

I'm making progress, I say.

He looks at me.

I'm getting a lot out of the therapy sessions with Eskild, I continue. I recognize some behavioural patterns I haven't previously been aware of.

He nods.

I've been a big burden for you to carry this summer, I say. I realize that.

He looks away.

I have been totally... I'm looking for the word. Cuckoooo, I say, when I finally find it.

I make a fluttering motion with my hand near my right ear.

He gazes at me, perhaps he smiles a little. I'm not sure.

Moving into your home was hard for me, I didn't really feel there was any room for me. I think I suspected you had only opened the door a crack.

He gives me an angry look.

But I handled it very poorly! I hasten to add. I was jealous of Emma because I felt you had opened the door wider for her.

He's cupping his glass of ginger tea with both hands. It's on the table.

Yes, you did, he says.

96

It was childish of me, I say.

For a while we remain silent.

Then he says:

It was a nice letter you sent to Oliver.

It warms my heart to hear it.

Have you read it? I say.

Yes, he says. It was really kind.

Thank you, I say.

In my letter to Oliver I wrote that I had behaved in a disgusting way that evening and had said awful things to him, which I regret and apologize for. I also wrote that I can understand why he had shouted that I was fucking insane. That my behaviour really was fucking insane. I tried to explain that when you act like that, it's not because you've made a choice to act like that. It's because there's something terribly wrong with your brain at that moment. And that I'm devouring all the therapy I can get so I'll never behave like that again. In closing, I wrote that those times when he came downstairs holding my concealer in his hand and asking me to cover up a pimple for him had made me very happy. The trust he had shown me had made me happy.

I say to Jan:

My psychiatrist says I have a mild form of borderline personality disorder.

He looks at me.

I'm going to get well again! I say.

Yes? he says.

When I'm well, I continue, should we try again?

He starts gathering up his things.

No, he says.

It feels as if I'm spilling out of my body, right through my anus.

Why? I say.

He gets up from his chair.

Because by then a year will have probably passed and I'll have moved on.

The anxieties begin snapping at me like rats.

I'm so angry with you! he says.

I can understand that, I say.

We stand face to face. He briefly puts his hands around my shoulders. And then he leaves.

I grab my coat and walk back to the apartment in Sankt Hans Gades Passage. I turn on P1 and begin unpacking the bag of clothes he has brought.

In the bottom of the bag is a smaller bag. It contains all my panties. He has folded them neatly. Like they do in the lingerie display at Magasin department store. White, black, red, beige lace. Meticulously folded, stacked, and carefully slipped into the little bag.

I believe I'll get him back, I think.

Sønder Vilstrup, Jutland
The 1970s

There are rules:

Only the dining room is heated (by means of a wood-burning stove, and it's very cold until an hour after we have lit the fire upon returning from school). We're not particularly poor, but you become sluggish from too much heat and from long, hot showers. The other rooms are freezing cold. There are frost patterns on the inside of the windows. Water that accumulates in the saucer under the leaking radiator forms a thin, icy membrane. The water heater is lit on Saturdays when everyone takes a shower. You're not allowed to sleep in, not even on the weekend. You economize with the margarine for frying, and therefore you're not to wash the pans after use (the margarine can be reused for the next time). When you pull out the pans, there are usually thin parallel tracks in the margarine, created by two mouse teeth. You don't listen to mindless pop music on P3 and you don't watch profit-driven American movies. You're not to watch TV in the first place, apart from Fassbinder, *The Emigrants*, *Buddenbrooks*, films by Bergman, programs on foreign politics. For that very reason the televison set is in the ice-cold dining room where the saucer of water is located.

Niels and I sneak in there sometimes and lie down on the corner sofa that our father has built. We crawl under the blankets and turn the TV on at a low volume because my father's study is right above us. The programs we like the best are those that are listed as B/W in the TV guide.

It's not until many years later that we find out it means black and white, but it is irrelevant to us as we don't have a colour TV, and besides, the B/W films *are* the best: Laurel and Hardy, for instance, or Westerns, preferably with John Wayne, who my mother likes. There's something about his eyes, she says, he knows a thing or two about women, she adds. I'm mostly fascinated by the Indigenous People, I'm on their side. I very much want to be a Native American, I'm always crazily in love with the wildest of the men, my stomach does flip-flops, and I love it when he rides bareback and reins in his mustang at the top of a cliff above the plains that are unfolding below him. Sometimes I watch the credits and look for his real name on the list of actors and write it down just in case I should be lucky enough to track him down someday.

There are also rules that happen ad hoc. Those are the most difficult because they demand you're constantly on your toes and able to anticipate what will happen next.

First of all, you have to be able to put two and two together and understand that since your father doesn't care for long, warm baths and mindless American TV, he won't like *Golden Love Tales* either, the magazine that Anne has a whole box of hidden under her bed upstairs in the old servant's room on the far side of the loft. Second, you have to keep an eye on him so you can stop doing or saying whatever you're doing or saying if the skin around his eyes begins to twitch, and they get hard, and the corners of his mouth turn down in a mocking way. If you don't manage to stop in time, the story ends with 1) him shouting and maybe throwing stuff at you or running after you, or 2) him ridiculing you.

At times I need my father to be away. So then I ask, when the five of us are sitting down eating supper, what plans he has for the next while, if he has any meetings coming up in Copenhagen or something. If he says yes, I take on a serious expression, squirm a bit and say: Aw.

When the cat's away, the mice will eat more than the margarine in the frying pan. That's when we—Niels, Anne, my mother, and I—walk over to Bent Shopkeeper, who for now is cordiality itself, but years later will hang himself in the back room. He stands behind the counter, wrings his hands, and says, How-mayihelpyou?

When my father is away, soya pâté and vegetables and whole grain bread are not on our shopping list. Instead we buy a large loaf of white bread sprinkled with poppy seeds, three cans of mackerel in tomato sauce, and a tube of mayonnaise. And then we laugh and talk while hurrying back the one and a half kilometres from Bent Shopkeeper to our farmhouse. We take turns carrying the bag, it's not a big deal. And once we're at home, we get to work:

We slice the bread, boil some eggs, set out four plates on the kitchen table, distribute the bread among the four plates. First the mackerel in tomato sauce is placed on the bread, then the egg, then salt, and finally mayonnaise. The whole menagerie is then carried to the room with the TV. We consume everything. All the programs until there aren't any more—and all the white bread.

Vesterbrogade, Copenhagen
November 2015

I'm at a shawarma bar in Vesterbro with Malte and Anne when the text message comes in.

It feels nice being with them. I'm eating a bit.

Then my mobile dings. I dig it out of my purse.

What kind of jackass is that man anyway, your ex! I just saw him on Tinder. Jeez, that didn't take him long. Hugs, Esther.

I don't know how many times you can spill out of yourself. It's happening again. My anus expands, and I drop out.

He's desperate, Malte says.

I turn into the tiny point that's staring out through the holes in my eyes.

I call Ida when I'm back in my apartment by Sankt Hans Torv. She says:

Don't worry about it, Karen, the only thing that might happen if he meets another woman is that he'll soon be missing you.

From past experience I know I'll believe anything Ida says.

Sankt Hans Gade Passage
Nørrebro Neighbourhood in Copenhagen
Nights
November 2015

I'm able to fall asleep. The hippie psychiatrist has given me sleeping pills.

But I bolt awake after three hours. Every night. My fucked-up life is a train wreck. I suffer from love anxiety. At no point do I see any possibility of the illness disappearing unless Jan returns.

I stare into the darkness. Eskild has told me that the psychotic state I was in when committed has settled in my body in the form of stress. Much of it is pure physiology, he says, powerful hormonal surges. I assume that it'll take up to half a year before your pulse will slow down and for your body to relax.

I get up, go to the kitchen, put on the kettle for tea. Bring the radio over to the mattress on the floor. Turn on P1. Sit down with my back against the wall. I seldom cry, never during the night. I stare into space.

After a couple of hours I may lie down again, with a pillow between my knees so they won't get sore.

Psychotherapy Outpatient Clinic
Ballerup, Greater Copenhagen Area
November 2015

As a child I was the person my father preferred on a day-to-day basis. It came back to me when the hippie psychiatrist firmly established my diagnosis. A diagnosis is an identity. The only thing is, my diagnosis lacks an identity.

I mention it to Eskild. I'm staggering around without an identity in a diagnostic cage that ironically signals identity loss, I say.

He sits across from me in his narrow office. A student is seated at the end of this intestinal tube of a room. She doesn't take her eyes off me. I'm used to being watched. That's what they do in psychiatry. Observing, it's called. She keeps an eye on everything I say and do. Searching for signs of insanity. I take no notice of her, have put all shame behind me. Shame is a First World problem.

Eskild smiles. Then he says:

Now, clearly, diagnoses are not a buffet from which you can pick and choose.

Pussy Galore Restaurant
Sankt Hans Torv
Nørrebro Neighbourhood in Copenhagen
November 2015

I spread out my clothes on the mattress so I can choose the right combination. Jan has agreed to meet me at Pussy Galore to give me more clothes. I feel dizzy and don't know if it's because I'm sick or because I'm hungry. I explore the latter possibility first and go to the kitchen and open the fridge. There's only some Icelandic skyr and skimmed milk. I take out the skyr and scoop two tablespoons into a bowl. Put the tablespoon in the sink and take out a teaspoon. I sit down at the small table in the kitchen, my legs folded under me, and begin. Half a teaspoon at a time. I close my eyes. Force half of it down my throat, then give up and decide to take a shower.

I force myself to enjoy the water. Try to relax the muscles in my face. Open my mouth. Close my eyes, letting the water run down my hair and my face, letting it seep in between my lips. I press my fingers lightly against my body, my belly, my armpits. My armpits have changed. Now I can clearly feel my skeleton here as well.

I wrap my hair in one towel and my body in another. Sit down on the kitchen chair to ease the dizziness. Drink water. After a while I manage to get up again and start applying makeup. I don't think of anything other than the pleasant picture I'm making appear in the mirror. The black lines I'm drawing around my eyes. The mascara. The pauses along the way when I lean against the wall to support myself. My pulse that has been racing constantly since my hospital admission. Now and again I press two fingers against my carotid artery to feel its impressive speed.

At 4:25 in the afternoon I leave the apartment and walk the two hundred metres to Sankt Hans Torv.

When I reach the square, I can see Jan. He's standing outside Pussy Galore, looking in my direction. I'm conscious of my gait, want it to seem fluid and with a springy step, I want to approach him relaxed, drift toward him, preferably appearing a bit sexy.

He gives me one of his quick kisses on the cheek, which hurts, and we go inside. The bartender is a young man with a beard. I send him a smile, thinking that no one can blame me for flirting since I don't have a boyfriend. But all I wish is that Jan will notice that the bartender is flirting back.

We order coffee and sit at a table in the back of the room. I smile, courteous, it's paramount that I give the impression of being well, of looking strong, sweet, and intelligent. And beautiful. I'm selling myself as a woman. Evidently it's going according to plan. I'm wearing a short dress, and every time I change position and place one thigh over the other, he follows the movements of my legs. Not with a quick sidelong glance. His gaze is persistent. The same with my hands that move around in the space between us. He follows them. And my lips. I once read in a women's magazine that if a man's gaze constantly slides from the woman's eyes to her lips, it's because he desires her.

At last we hold each other's gaze. I've seen this expression in his eyes before. I recognize it from when his sex swells and becomes erect. I know he's sitting on the other side of the table with a semi-stiff dick, and I feel ecstatic.

He has forgotten my clothes.

That's a good sign.

We decide that I'll come to his place and pick them up on Saturday.

After he has left, I don't go home. I run down to Anne's at Sortedam Dossering. Shuffle my feet in the cold while waiting for her to open the door. Slip quickly past her and step inside.

Karen, she says.

I lean against the wall in the entrance hall.

It's very strange, I say.

Yes? she says.

I tell her the whole thing.

Yes, that's very strange, she says.

If I didn't know any better, I say, if I knew for sure that I could trust my intuition, I would say that Jan is still in love with me.

Viborg, Jutland
The 1970s

When we go to visit my paternal grandparents in Viborg, I have to wear the woollen knickers they gave me for Christmas. They are dark green and buttoned up just below the knee, so you have to wear long, heavy stockings as well. I think they look weird, and moreover, they are scratchy.

The atmosphere in the car is tense. It always is when we drive to Viborg unless it's just a stopover on our way to my other grandparents who live farther north in Vendsyssel. My father is edgy, his thumb turning and turning in its socket. I sit in the middle on the back seat of our Volvo 544 with one leg on either side of the drive-shaft hump; hence I can see his thumb move around on the steering wheel.

We feel sorry for our father. He has told us he's edgy because my grandfather used to pull out his leather belt with a snap and beat him with it. And because they always argue about politics. My father is a socialist and has disgraced the family. Only his younger sister understands him. For she's become a socialist too.

You inherit things from your family. Height and weight, for instance. In my father's family, you inherit insanity.

There have been several insane people in the family, my grandmother's mother being one of them. Helga was her name.

She became increasingly unstable to the point where she was committed repeatedly to an insane asylum. She was manic depressive. Inheriting from her is what we fear the most.

She came from a cultured home associated with the folk high school movement and married Vilhelm, who was a liberal politician and a sand-dune inspector in Vejers on the west coast. An honest and practical man, they say. So Helga moved from the fertile east Jutland to the bleak west Jutland where the wind had knocked over the few remaining trees. But Helga missed her trees and flowers and didn't feel well overall, so Vilhelm dropped everything he was doing and began sowing and planting all around the dune-inspector's house that sat on the barren, sandy soil right behind the dunes. He succeeded in forcing beech trees, honeysuckle, and roses out of the sand and planting flowerbeds with willowherbs, lady's mantle, and crane's bill. All of it to make Helga happier.

That's love, my father says.

And it was so remarkable that the king himself came to see the garden. But Vilhelm's efforts could not save Helga.

She died in 1912 at the age of forty at Middelfart Hospital for the Insane. Some people say she took her own life. Now she rests by the little church in the naked landscape in the middle of Oksbøl military firing range with its soot-smeared houses and windows boarded up with bullet-riddled plywood, and the rumbling noise from artillery being fired across the heath. A bleak place like this is where you might end up if you're insane. This much I know.

It's from my father's mother and Helga and Helga's father that my love of music and literature originates, and my father tells me one shouldn't be ashamed of mental illness. It often goes together with art and sensitivity and talent.

But he's afraid. Afraid he'll be the one to pass it on. For sure, it won't be his younger brother. He's a nuclear physicist, which is more down to earth than an artist, and he didn't become a socialist either, putting the family to shame.

It's a good thing adding some grounding to the clan's sensitive, artistic side, something I sense early on. My mother is like that, down to earth and capable, my father says.

My mother tells me:

Karina! Keeping your feet on the ground will serve you best.[3]

Or:

Karina, tread the boards with care, for the stage is sloped![4]

My father's father is also grounded. He was director of the Asmildkloster Agricultural College, which looms large on the far side of Lake Nørresø in Viborg, that's where my father grew up, but now his parents live in a big house with a beautiful garden that slopes down to the lake from where you can see a cathedral on the other side.

The house is grand inside. Shiny mahogany furniture with inlays, silver cutlery nestled in green felt within the sideboard's shallow drawers in the dining room. Paintings. Books. My grandfather's heavy desk with his fountain pen and ink pot. His Knight's Cross of the Order of the Dannebrog. The candy tin that we steal from. The little bamboo table that is brought in and placed next to my grandfather at the head of the table from which he hands out beer and pop.

If you give my grandmother a drawing or a horse chestnut you've made into a spider by attaching machsticks for legs and then wrapped in yarn to simulate a spiderweb, she'll stop what she's doing and praise your creation. She'll describe in her own words the thing you have made, and I'll feel proud and warm inside and feel the desire to make things and share them with my grandmother. With my grandmother and my father. He does the same thing when I show him my drawings—puts everything aside and spends a long time looking at them. Of the grandchildren, I'm the best artist, and I tape sheets of paper together to make large surfaces to draw on, and I sketch entire towns full of people and markets, and there is no one I would rather give my drawings to than those two people .

My father's parents were born in the 1880s, which explains some of these things. We discuss it on our way back home in the Volvo, with Linka lying in the front. And it's really difficult for them to understand that my father ended up being a socialist with his long hair covering his ears, my mother adds.

Lyngby, Greater Copenhagen Area
November 2015

On the S-train from Nørreport out to Jan's place in Lyngby, I have a long, reprimanding conversation with myself. I use harsh words and make it clear to myself that what happened at Pussy Galore the other day was a one-off episode. He had been overcome by the situation, but now has had time to think it over and come to his senses and regain his self-control. I'll be met with a cool kiss on the cheek and a look you give neighbours, dogs, and people you have let go of.

I stop on the platform in Lyngby. Dig out the benzodiazepines from my purse. Break the tiny pill in two pieces and chew one of them. I lessen my chances if he senses my nervousness. But I shouldn't appear dopey either. That would be really stupid.

On my way to the row house, I stop several times. Get going again. Stop again. It's possible that he may see me from the kitchen window when I walk up the path, so when I turn by the hedge and potentially enter his field of vision, all my attention is focused on my gait and movements.

I don't see him in the kitchen window. I stop by the front door. Then I put one foot up on the step, lean forward and ring the doorbell, and step back again, so when he opens the door I won't be standing right outside it. But at a distance. So he will be able to see my entire body.

The door opens. Jan looks at me. He's smiling.

Karen, he says. Hi.

In one catlike movement I step up to the threshold, say hi, and walk inside.

Jan touches my cheek with his lips. They remain there long enough for me to feel their warmth. He pulls me closer and gives me a hug.

I've made us some coffee, he says.

That sounds nice, I say, and do my best to hide how overwhelmed I feel while I unwind my scarf, hang it up, and take my coat off. I sense he's looking at me when I stretch to reach the coat hook.

He has set the table for us in the living room. There is bread and cheese on the table, plates and cups and knives. P8 Jazz is on.

I sit at the side of the table that faces the narrow garden.

The light is nice and bright today, I say, pointing at the garden.

We cut back the tall, crowded trees shortly before I moved out so I could enjoy the light and see a bit of sky.

Jan pours my coffee and passes me the basket with the buns he has baked.

I ask about his work, about Oliver, his mother. He asks how things are with me. We don't talk about illness and hospitals. We discuss the essay about Lisbon that I've just finished and for which he has contributed photos.

That was fun, he says.

I nod.

We made many plans about the articles I had to write and the accompanying photographs you had to take, I say, smiling.

He looks down into his lap and smiles. Then he looks up.

Yes, he says.

We're silent.

I place my hand, palm up, in the middle of the table while looking at him.

I hear him breathe, a strong exhalation passes through his nose. As if his soul is escaping. He lifts his hand and places it on top of mine. I wrap my fingers around it, and he lets me. We sit like that for a while, smiling shyly.

Nothing else happens, so I get up, walk past him and upstairs to the bathroom. I have already planned that when I come back I'll walk over and stand next to him to see if he'll reach for me.

When I come downstairs again, I walk toward him. His back is facing me. I stand close behind him, my arms hanging by my sides. He turns to me and places a hand on my hip and strokes it with his thumb. I put my hand on his shoulder, everything is happening very slowly, time seems impeded by a built-in resistance. As if we with our slow movements are pressing against an elastic membrane.

Then I swing one leg across him and straddle his lap, facing him, the membrane bursts.

He pulls me closer, puts his hands in my hair, grabs me around my waist, my ass, clumsy, chaotic movements, I cup his face in my hands, kiss him. He's trembling. His entire body is shaking violently. He gets up under me, we tear our clothes off, they lie spread out like a trail of blood, and we tumble onto the bed in the next room. My body leans back toward the mattress, and his follows, all in one movement. My lip is bleeding and I notice blood on his shoulder and chest. He's between my thighs, and his dick enters me almost before my back hits the sheet.

He looks down at my face, fondly, smiling. My fingers stroke his eyes, lips.

PART
THREE

The Harbourfront at Islands Brygge in Copenhagen
January 2016

I have obtained an apartment in Gunløgsgade that I can sublet for five months. It has a bay window, and when I stand in front of it, I can see the water by the harbourfront and the sky above it. In the evenings I see the lights in the windows of the hotels and office buildings on Kalvebod Brygge across the harbour, and Jan when he comes around the corner on his bike.

I open the door for him, and we stand holding each other for a long time.

It's a good thing you waited for us, he says in my ear.

We buy a book called *The Hungry Heart*. It's written by a journalist whose wife has borderline personality disorder. It doesn't describe us as manipulative lunatics but as human beings who are sensitive and have more mood swings and bouts of abandonment anxiety than most people.

Concurrently I read Carsten René Jørgensen's book on personality disorders.[5] It's a knowledge-rich, academic work, but at the same time he tries to describe BPD as seen from within.

I get the feeling I could easily curl up and place myself in his hands. He writes that one of the central characteristics of people with BPD is an awareness of not having an authentic connection to the world while at the same time having a strong desire to establish contact with the world and other people. We yearn desperately to belong. And we often feel we're dominated by our need to experience love and we have a tendency to be overwhelmed by our immediate impulses. He writes of impulses that often involve a desire for life but are typically self-destructive. BPD is the mental illness with the highest suicide rate because the disorder itself causes so much anguish. The fundamental emotions are loneliness, emptiness, and the feeling of being shut out. Or of never really feeling part of the human family in the first place, he writes.

Jan and I go for long walks in the evening. We walk along the harbourfront toward the neighbourhood of Christianshavn, stop for a coffee at Freetown Christiania, continue to the former dockyards at Holmen or across the bike bridge to the Playhouse and the canal area of Nyhavn, walk back via Kalvebod Brygge and across the other bike bridge by Fisketorvet Shopping Mall in the harbour district. Or we walk down along the wharf, through Nokken's quaint allotment gardens and farther south to Sluseholmen and back up to Fisketorvet and the bridge.

We hold hands as we walk and try to come to terms with the fact that I have an overwhelming need to feel loved and stable in our relationship. While he has an enormous need to be free and not have to commit himself to meet up on a regular basis. Closeness and strong attachments to others weigh him down. And his need to keep his distance and not fully commit to me, and to us, weighs me down.

It's almost a Gordian knot, I say.

He doesn't answer.

Sometimes I get the feeling you're sizing me up, I say. I long for the day you want to devour me without hesitation.

Except that's not who I am, he says.

No, I say, I know.

But could you perhaps indulge me and text me twice on the days we're not together? And say good morning and good night?

Okay, I can do that, he says.

Sønder Vilstrup, Jutland
The 1970s

It's possible that you have what's called "early trauma," my mother says when I'm nine and she has begun studying to be an early childhood educator.

She looks concerned, but I think it sounds exciting. I feel like I'm something special. My mother is taking developmental psychology at the college of education, and she tells me that one's personality is formed in early childhood. She tells me that very small children have "separation anxiety." I'm not used to hearing my mother use these kinds of words. She tells me I probably suffered separation anxiety when I was eight months old and Anne and I were left with our grandparents in Vendsyssel and didn't see our parents again till three months later, and then, upon our return, they had enough to do caring for my sick brother who died one month later.

She tells me my father had to do his job at Askov Højskole, and she had to live in a tent at a campground in Aarhus while Jens was treated at the Radiation Centre.

She could have told me anything, nothing makes sense to me. I know it would have been appropriate to express pity for a baby experiencing separation anxiety, but in my mind I only see what Anne had told me about the blood pouring out of Jens's nose when he threw up. And I don't like the words *Radiation Centre*.

The Harbourfront at Islands Brygge in Copenhagen
January 2016

I've started eating again. Which worries me. The anxiety disappeared the day Jan came back. But I got hungry.

It feels as if a foreign object has been planted inside my stomach, a vacuum with a powerful suction that extends beyond my mouth. Bread and meat stick to my lips with such intensity that I can't stop them from entering. But I can still feel my skeleton when I press my fingers against my armpit.

Jan loves my thin body. In the evening I lie down carefully on the bed in a black bra and lace panties. He leans over me, watching me. His gaze is a thread that slowly moves across my body, from my instep to my shin, knee, thigh, hip, stomach, chest, neck, shoulder, along my arm to my hand and fingers that are resting on the sheet.

You're so beautiful, sweetie, he whispers, while he eases off my panties. I'm so delicate that these kinds of things must be done with great care.

He moves a little to get a better view of my stomach and pubis with the triangle that I adjust each and every day. His fingers slide down to the labia that I laboriously rub with lotion every day after having shaved them completely smooth.

You are exquisite, he says.

I lie very still, letting him gaze at me and letting him caress my body ever so slowly.

I love being his exquisite little girl, and I'm terrified of my hunger.

Sønder Vilstrup, Jutland
1976

We always keep an ear out for our mother and father. And once they begin arguing, we come out of our rooms. Niels and I settle at the top of the stairs and watch them down below. Anne goes all the way downstairs. She confronts them, straightens her back, and proceeds to tell them to behave and act like adults. Sometimes she succeeds. At other times my father throws things around, and my mother yells and cries. I know that children don't like it when their parents argue, but I do. It brings us all together.

The Harbourfront at Islands Brygge in Copenhagen
February 2016

We, the hippie psychiatrist and I, think I have an eating disorder. I'm excessively focused on being thin, we suspect. Atypical bulimia. The atypical part is my inability to throw up. I can't figure out how to do it. I've tried bending over the toilet with a finger down my throat, but the only thing that comes out of me are terrible sounds. So I compensate, as they call it, by running and walking and doing CrossFit workouts. And periodically by going without eating. Until I can't fend off the suction in my stomach, and I throw myself on food, drooling and slobbering.

On those days I don't go out. On those days I don't brush my teeth, don't wear a bra, I stink, and the discharge between my legs leaves greasy tracks on the floor. I eat and I eat and hate myself, and there's food on my naked breasts, and they swell from inside of me and turn into lumps of flesh hanging from my skeleton, the wonderful skeleton I long for that is my real self.

I'm granted permission to receive treatments for eating disorders at Stolpegård Psychotherapy Centre. My idea is to get my foot in the door so that I can also receive treatments for personality disorders there. For I have a hunch that the eating disorder is a river made up of tributaries, and the river can't be drained until the flow from the side streams is under control.

Comorbidity. I learned unpleasant words like this long ago. My eating disorder is a comorbid condition.

We treat the comorbid disorders first, they say at Stolpegård. We'll start with your eating disorder. After that you can receive treatments for your personality disorder.

I tell them I'd understand the sequence of treatments if, for instance, it were a case of life-threatening anorexia, but in my opinion, my eating disorder will not disappear until I:

- am able to write again
- can once again hear how Danish sentences are constructed when I translate
- have the courage to leave my apartment during daylight hours
- stop crossing to the other side of the street when somebody is approaching me
- feel that I'm part of the human family
- am brave enough to believe that Jan won't leave me should my skeleton be covered in flesh and fat

Can we start with that? I say.

We cannot.

The Harbourfront at Islands Brygge in Copenhagen
April 2016

I google things. I have an ongoing investigation underway about mastering the art of suicide. I do thorough research, I don't want to risk botching it, either I'll succeed at first attempt or, at the very least, be able to carry on as before without brain damage or a broken back. I already have enough on my plate.

I tend toward the old tried-and-true method with a warm bath and booze and sleeping pills and razor blades. It'll take place in a hotel. I want to spare my children from having to see that version of me.

The Harbourfront at Islands Brygge in Copenhagen
May 2016

Even the smallest thing can seem insurmountable. Doing the dishes, for instance. There's no dishwasher in the apartment, so cups and glasses pile up on the kitchen counter.

Jan helps me when he comes over. He does the washing, and I the drying.

We laugh about it. We joke that he's my support person and I'm his client. He has been a support worker for people with mental illness in the past. Helped out with their dishes.

We frequently meet at Fitness dk by Vesterport Station. Sometimes we just work out and have a quick cup of coffee after, at other times he comes back to my place and sleeps over.

I know I ought to be happy and bubbly when we finally meet. But I'm often sad and brooding.

It's difficult for me to handle the in-between times, I say during one of our breaks.

We stand face-to-face in the CrossFit area.

He looks apprehensive, something he usually does when I talk about how I feel.

It's difficult for me to say goodbye to you, I elaborate, and get used to being alone. And difficult to see you again after several days have passed.

He stares at me.

I'm not very flexible by nature, I say apologetically.

But I don't know what to do, he says, and gives me a worried look.

Actually, I think the biggest help you can give me when I'm feeling this way is just to hold me, I say quietly.

The anxious look disappears from his eyes. He reaches for me and holds me tight.

It feels as if I've escaped a narrow intestine inside myself and emerged into the open air where I can once again move my arms, lift my head, and look around me.

I watch him jump up and grab hold of a steel bar that's suspended from the ceiling, then raise and lower himself, over and over again.

We cycle across Langebro to get to my place but notice the soft light by Bryggen. We park the bikes and sit down on the wharf by Kulturhuset, our legs dangling above the water. I'm drinking alcohol-free beer. I don't dare drink alcohol any longer, I haven't since my hospitalization. I have to stay sharp and alert.

He lies down on his back, his legs still dangling above the water.

I wonder why everything is a bit lopsided, I say.

He smiles and shrugs. Looks me in the eye.

I touch the lopsided parts. The cleft in his chin that is a tiny bit off centre, the nose with its little tilt, the upper lip that pulls upward on one side, and the twisted eye tooth behind it. All of it pulls to the same side.

He lies completely still and looks at me.

It's very sexy, I say, very attractive.

He lifts his hand and takes hold of my hair.

I've never had a girlfriend who could see me so clearly, he says. And I don't mean just my face.

He turns on his side and pulls me down beside him. His hand is still in my hair, we kiss, for a long time, and his body begins to tremble, I can feel it everywhere, in his hand that cups the back of my head, in his chest, his belly, his thighs, he leans his head back a shade, and his lip pulls upward even further.

It all happens so subtly that no one notices, we are just two people who lie in the sun kissing each other.

He opens his eyes and looks at me tenderly.

I had an orgasm, he says.

I stare at him, surprised.

I had no idea you could have an orgasm without ejaculating, I say, and look at him wide-eyed. And without me touching your dick at all.

It's new for me too, he says, and smiles.

We gather our things and push our bikes toward Gunløgsgade. We hold hands. Laugh. I remember something Ida says, that with me sadness and joy are often right next to each other.

Søerne — The City Lakes in Copenhagen
May 2016

Anne and I are on one of our many walks around all three lakes at dusk. Always in the same direction and with the same side trips, just to gain a few additional metres and avoid the places with the worst traffic. We walk at a fair clip while talking.

When I'm not able to write, I feel I shall die, I say to her.

At first she doesn't answer. Then she says:

That's not good, Karen.

No, I say.

Anne is walking with a slight stoop, she does that when she's thinking.

Would it make sense to you, she says, if we agree to an arrangement where you send me something written, a text, at regular intervals?

Yes? I say, and slow down.

She turns to face me.

Yes! I say.

Then I can give you some feedback every time you send me something?

I stop walking. Look intensely at her.

Yes, I repeat. It would be fantastic if you have the energy for it.

Anne starts walking again.

That's what we'll do then.

Thank you! I say, and start walking as well.

Twice a week? she says. Mondays and Thursdays?

Yes, please, I say, wrapping my arm around her shoulder.

Anne is an associate professor in comparative literature. I feel I can trust what she has to say.

But you must be honest, I say. And tell me if it's a pile of shit.

I promise, she says.

But perhaps say it in a gentle way, especially in the beginning, I say, so I won't feel too defeated.

That's settled then, she says.

And perhaps mention if there's something you think is working well, I say.

Of course, she says.

I start writing again. I write every day. Some days three lines, other days six or eight. I write about my stay at the Psychiatric Centre in Ballerup and send a little sample off to Anne every Monday and Thursday. An hour after I've sent it, I receive an answer. She thinks it's working out. I forget that I can't write.

Frederiksberg Neighbourhood in Copenhagen and Vangede, Greater Copenhagen Area
The end of June 2016

I have my own apartment now. I can stay put there. There's room for Selma too. It's on the top floor, with a view of Frederiksberg Hospital's old buildings. Outside the windows in the living room is the sky. Sunlit rectangles are projected on the floorboards. In the evening airplanes drag pink stripes behind them across roofs and chimneys. On windless days they puff up and hang like unravelled intestines in the sky.

Once again there's no language inside me. I don't know how sentences are put together. Neither when I write nor when I translate. I'm scared that my language won't ever return. I don't know how I can earn money if I can't hear the language.

For the first time in my life I've decided to apply for public support so I can get better under more peaceful and calm conditions.

The reply arrives in my municipal eBox. It says I most likely won't be eligible to receive sickness benefits but instead will be considered for integration assistance intended for persons who have been out of the country for a certain number of months in the past eight years.

I jump up and start pacing up and down. I scratch my arm with my fingernails. It's impossible to see how I can make ends meet.

I spend the next couple of days pacing in the apartment. One day a kitchen knife appears on the floor in front of me, its point embedded in the wood. I don't remember how it ended up there. I make appointments. During the hours leading up to the appointments I walk back and forth, trying to figure out how to get dressed. How to propel myself out the door.

But today I manage to get dressed. I'm off to group therapy at Stolpegård Psychotherapy Centre in Vangede. The group for eating disorders. I walk down the stairs in the apartment building, holding on to the walls. I make out a small patch of each step in the space right in front of my eyes. I unlock my bicycle. I walk into Stolpegård. I don't remember how I got there. There's a wall. I lean against it. A partial face appears in front of me. I know whose face it is. It belongs to the therapist. I can hear what she's saying. She says it's not a good idea for me to join the group today. She says I have to see the psychiatrist whose office is farther down the hallway. She accompanies me to the door.

I'm told to sit on a chair in the psychiatrist's office. She makes calls to various hospitals. She tells me she would like to have me admitted. She says I'm suicidal. She says I'm not psychotic. I reply in an appropriate manner without prolonged response time, as it's called in neuropsychology. She says I'm depressive. She doesn't want me to go to the Psychiatric ER at Bispebjerg first. She wants me to be admitted directly to the closed ward at Frederiksberg, she says. She apologizes for sitting with her back turned toward me while making the calls. She asks if I would rather wait outside while she makes the calls.

A taxi is coming, she says. It can take my bicycle too.

The Closed Ward
Frederiksberg Hospital, Copenhagen
The end of June 2016

I ring the doorbell at the closed ward. A male care worker unlocks the door and offers me his hand.

Are you Karen? he says.

Yes.

We don't go directly into the closed ward. First we have to go through a secure, locked room. It has another door in addition to the one we've just entered. He locks it behind us. I'm one of those who needs to be locked up.

I'm being told to place my bag on a table. A female care worker is present. She shakes my hand. They open the bag. I'm standing in the middle of the floor. They empty the bag. Out come gym clothes, computer, cellphone, cables for the computer and phone, hairbrush, hairspray. Maybe I had hoped for a day at the fitness centre and a place to sit with my computer. They keep the cables and the hairspray. The rest they put back in the bag.

I'm well aware of why they take the cables. But I don't understand how I could kill myself with hairspray. They unlock the second door. I'm afraid. I don't know what to expect once I'm on the other side of the door. Not having been in a closed ward before.

Eyes turn in my direction and look me over when I step over the threshold from the secure room to the ward. A man in a wheelchair is parked in the wide hallway I now find myself in. He's wearing a hospital shirt on one arm and shoulder. A pair of large white underpants with a green stripe and the Capital Region logo has slipped off his butt and hangs from his thighs. I can see his grey pubic hair and his dick, a wrinkly flap of skin. I wonder what it smells like.

We enter a room next to where he's sitting. There's only one bed. It has a metal frame with straps in case you have to be restrained. There's one window. It's sealed. It occurs to me that spray bottles are a type of offensive weapon.

There's a large common room in the middle of the ward. I enter it. I bring my computer. I sit down at a table. A man is sitting in the corner, his heavy black bangs reach halfway down his nose. There's a narrow gap in his bangs, and I can make out one of his eyes, which constantly follows me. He could be one of those I have to watch out for. I pretend I'm doing something on my computer, but I'm really keeping an eye on things, trying to get an idea of whether anyone in the room is dangerous.

I can't get onto Capital Region's network. There is free wi-fi, so it ought to be possible. The others sit in front of the tv watching something very loud. Nevertheless, I ask no one in particular if they know anything about why it's so difficult to get onto the network. Everyone turns around. I'm looking at seven faces. Then two of them actually get up and walk over to me. The younger one bends over my Mac and suggests various things, but they don't really work. The other one, judging from his facial features might be from Bosnia or Serbia, somewhere in the Balkans in any case, and when he speaks I'm certain for his accent is obvious. He says different things that don't make sense to me, and he's terribly nervous.

Now I'm the one who's dangerous.

But he succeeds in guiding me through a process that ends with Capital Region's network suddenly opening for me. I thank him profusely, and he twists and pulls on his beard and smiles. I also give thanks to the other faces that look at us from the couch by the TV.

Sønder Vilstrup, Jutland
The 1970s

My father is the one who comes to my room when I cry in the evening after having gone to bed. He sits by my bedside. He's sad, I can see that, and I feel sorry for him. He has a story he tells me when I'm sad about being bullied in school. It's Karen Blixen's tale about life that may seem meaningless and painful but that in the end turns out to be a perfect, beautiful image, a stork. He says the suffering we humans feel is part of the design that makes up our lives, that makes our lives rich.[6] But you cannot see it when you're in the middle of it. You need distance to see that stork. It helps when he sits with me. But I don't feel that the talk about the stork helps. I only wish something could be done so the kids at school would want to hang out with me.

When you're a newcomer, you'll be teased at school. That's clear to me. Newcomers are different. We're different because we have two old Volvo 544s with adhesive stickers on the rear window: *Renewable Energy* and *No to Nuclear Power*. We're different because we have a grand piano in the living room. We're different because we have books. We're different because we lived in big army tents when they were building Kolding Højskole, and bare-breasted women with trowels in their belts came from Aalborg and Copenhagen,[7] and we're different because we listen to the progressive Swedish Hoola Bandoola Band, Bob Dylan, the

Freetown Christiana album and the Woodstock album, and because we participate in demonstrations, we follow them, especially the anti-nuclear ones, but also Solvognen, with their horses and activists dressed up as North American Indigenous Peoples. We're different because we're communists. Although I'm not completely sure we're actually communists.

The Closed Ward
Frederiksberg Hospital, Copenhagen
The end of June 2016

In the evening I go outside to the area enclosed by a tall wire fence that slopes inward at the top. Perhaps the sloping wires are there to make it even harder to climb the fence.

I've set my sights on a chair, but I discover that the eye behind the black bangs has picked out the very same spot. I stop and ask him if it's his chair. But it isn't, he'll take the other one over there, he says, pointing at a chair by the fence. Thank you, I say, we do a lot of thanking when hospitalized, we regress all the way back to our squeaky-clean childhood when we were out with our mother and knew how to behave. And yet some of us might suddenly decide to throw all proper behaviour to the wind and pick up chairs and plastic cutlery in our battle against civility.

But until then we observe formalities to the extreme.

A woman is sitting in the enclosed yard talking with her visitor.

It's lonely being mentally ill, she says to him.

He doesn't answer.

We're almost always in another world from the rest of you, she says, and looks straight ahead, her eyes full of grief.

He takes her hand in his.

I want to hold hands too.

Jan is at Roskilde Music Festival.

Later in the evening a young female resident doctor wants to talk to me. I'm sitting on my bed. She sits down in the chair opposite me with a notepad in her lap and asks how I am.

I feel calmer now after being admitted here, I say, caught by surprise.

That's good, she says, we're looking after you.

I tell her I'm a tiny point inside my body that destroys everything for myself. That I write bad translations and am digging my own grave. The publishers will never use me again if I continue this way, I say.

She grabs the box of Kleenex beside her on the table and hands it to me.

And I'm not able to write, I continue. The whole purpose of my life is my writing. If I'm not writing, I have no raison d'être. And if I don't have any raison d'être, I shall die, I say.

Will you? she says.

Yes, I say.

She leans forward, closer to me. Says that I have to talk to a social worker. That I need help getting sickness benefits.

After she leaves, I lie down on my side under the blanket. The ward is quiet, but it's difficult falling asleep. I wonder if the others can sleep. I'm thinking about the visual artist Stense Andrea Lind-Valdan and her naked body that I see pictures of in my Facebook feed. Her slight body covered in blood or ink. A body that spills out of its own contours and floods into my feed. I get up and take a picture of the bed with the crumpled blanket, the metal frame designed for restraining belts, the sealed window. I post it on Facebook.

The next morning I'm woken up by a nursing assistant. She's standing by my bed.

Good morning, Karen, she says.

Good morning, I say.

Then she says:

The doctor on duty has cancelled your appointment with the social worker.

I sit up with a start.

Why? I say.

The doctor didn't think it was necessary, she says. You're going to talk to him instead.

In my medical file the doctor writes:

> At first the stage was set for an interview with the social worker, but it is a matter of a complex, prolonged social problem in that she reacts as soon as there are conditions attached to some benefits for which she is not entitled on account of her having been abroad for several years. Thus we are dealing with a prolonged social problem.

I go down to the interview room. In addition to the psychiatrist, a young nurse is present. The doctor is suntanned and wears boat shoes and no socks. He gives me a friendly smile and asks why I want to apply for sickness benefits. I tell him I've been sick for the past year.

He nods, lets me talk.

If I could only have a peaceful period of three months where I don't have to work, it would help a lot to get me well again, I say.

First we have a ten-minute-long conversation where the patient speaks very coherently and relevantly about the course of her illness [...] The patient recounts that she has a job as a translator of novels and that she is well aware of it going poorly, meaning she cannot produce good translations. She herself describes it as cognitive disturbances, and her attitude shows certain signs of projection and abdication of responsibility.

It's just that I've been referred to integration assistance, I say.

What's that? he says.

Before I can answer, he continues.

Is it because you have lived abroad and earned a lot of money and not paid taxes?

I look at him, surprised.

No, I say. It's a new law. It affects me because my ex was posted as an aid worker with Danida in East Africa, and I came along.

The doctor leans back in his chair and looks at me while I speak. But suddenly he moves forward and places his folded hands on the table.

Then he says:

Karen, now I'm going to pass the responsibility over to you.

He makes a gesture with his hands as if he's moving an object from his side of the table to my side.

Your rent is 6,300 kroner, he says, and you will get 5,000 kroner in integration assistance. Surely you can see it doesn't add up, can't you? It's your responsibility. You have to learn to take responsibility, Karen.

I get up. I'm about to suffocate, stifled in the mask he believes is me. I know it's my BPD diagnosis that does it. We're manipulative and avoid taking responsibility. According to the old definition of the illness. I can't breathe. I tear at the borderline mask and say he doesn't see *me* but an outdated description of my diagnosis.

I cry.

I don't want to talk with you, I shout.

He leans back in his chair and looks at me.

I'm on my way out the door. I stop and turn to face him.

I'm more than capable of taking responsibility, I shout. I've always taken care of myself.

During the second part of the interview the situation is redressed and the boundaries set, including directing the patient to face the realities [...] In this connection the patient shows signs of being intensely emotional and cries and indicates that we don't understand her, and that it's hurtful when we declare that she isn't mentally ill.

I run through the day room to get to my room, the others stand up with their arms hanging limp, their faces expressing fear. They stare at me. I pace back and forth between the bed and the desk. I scratch my arm. Cry. The anxiety beast squirms, takes over my organs, breathes through my mouth.

There's a knock on the door. It's the psychiatrist. Behind him is the nurse who was present at the interview. I sit down on the bed and rock back and forth.

The psychiatrist remains standing just inside the door.

Do you want to be discharged? he says.

I stare into the wall. I try to think clearly so I can decide what the wisest thing to do is: to stay here with him or be by myself in the apartment.

You have to answer me now, he says.

I look at him.

I'd like to stay here, I say. I'm afraid the suicidal thoughts will return, and right now only my children are in Copenhagen, all the others are on vacation.

...will for instance not give an answer to whether she wants to be discharged or not. She doesn't appear psychotic, and she ends up saying she will go home and commit suicide so that yours truly will feel really bad. Consequently she appears rather immature and tends to be easily offended and sensitive when relating to others. I have attempted to direct the patient to face her role in being hospitalized and also pointed out the importance of her co-operating with the personnel in charge...Subsequently she declares that she wants to be discharged, which then takes place...Although she has never made any concrete attempt to commit suicide, she has nevertheless followed a pattern of suicidal thoughts for many years in connection with boundaries being established when she feels wronged.

The patient cries after the interview and attempts comforting by the nurse [sic], but if she continues demanding to be discharged, she will indeed be discharged.

I see no reason for you to stay here, the doctor says.

I stand up.

I'm scared, I shout.

The nurse takes a step toward me.

I'm scared, I repeat, and look her in the eye.

The doctor leaves.

The nurse puts her arms around me.

Try breathing with me, Karen, she says.

The anxiety beast has taken over my breathing, and I cannot.

She releases me. I lean against the wall. She begins packing my things. Hangs the gym bag over my shoulder.

I don't feel good about you leaving now, she says.

The bag slides off my shoulder, and she lifts it back on.

You have the right to complain about the incident, she says.

I suddenly remember that Selma is on her way to visit me.

My daughter is on her way, I say. I don't want her to see me like this.

The nurse holds on to my arm. Unlocks the door with her other hand. She follows me with her eyes until I'm all the way out in the parking lot.

I turn toward the gate once I'm in the parking lot. The one that faces Nordre Fasanvej.

Please be late, Selma, I whisper.

I hear a door open behind me. The doctor from the ward and two younger doctors pass me and cross Road 5.

I see Selma walking through the gate.

Emergency Room, Admission
Bispebjerg Hospital, Copenhagen
July 2016

Before Jan went to Roskilde Festival, I had suggested that he install Snapchat on his phone so we could supplement the two daily text messages with a picture. But we must have misunderstood each other. Instead of two text messages plus a picture, I now receive one message and one picture.

When I got his morning greeting today, which was a photo of his camping spot, I replied that it wasn't how I had understood our agreement, and that I thought the arrangement was even worse than before. I would prefer a text rather than a photo, I wrote.

I'm on my way to Gentofte from Frederiksberg on my bike. I'm going to visit Carsten and Helene. Carsten has prepared lunch and has even asked if I'm a vegetarian or have any food allergies. They are in the process of organizing a fundraiser so I can keep my apartment in case I get on integration assistance, and now I'm on my way out there to thank them.

I hear a ding and stop to dig the mobile out of my purse. It's a text message from Jan. He writes:

I'm not sure I can live up to your expectations.

My pulse starts racing. I don't know if his message just refers to the two text messages or if it's in general. I get on my bike again and discover I've ended up in Vangede, close to Stolpegård Psychotherapy Centre. What the fuck am I doing here? I'm biking with my head in the clouds.

I'm a receptacle for anxiety. I'm a receptacle for suicide. The two of them have combined to form a chemical compound of such high intensity that I have to tilt my head back to breathe enough oxygen. I cry and talk to myself while biking.

I turn around and head for Bispebjerg Hospital.

In my purse I carry the CRISIS PLAN that I compiled with the people at Stolpegård. It says on it that it's in my purse. And then it says that if I have suicidal thoughts I should:

1) exercise
2) take a warm bath
3) go for a walk or phone a) Anne or b) Ida or c) Niels.

If everything goes haywire, I should:

1) phone the Psychiatric ER at Frederiksberg Hospital, or
2) go directly to the Psychiatric ER at Bispebjerg Hospital.

That's where I am now.

I'm afraid they won't admit me. When they look up my file and see my diagnosis, they'll turn me away. I'm a person who play-acts and manipulates.

A nurse types in my ID number. She has looked me up now, but she nevertheless gets up and comes out to see me. She leads me by my shoulder, and we walk into the waiting room full of people and further on into a small screened-off space without people. I'm told to sit down on a chair. She puts a box of Kleenex on the table in front of me. She squats down next to me. Her arm is resting on the table beside the wet tissues.

She says:

It's not right that anyone should feel as bad as you do now. No one should be that unhappy.

I don't understand what's happening. She talks to me the way one talks to ordinary people. She believes I'm genuinely unhappy. That I'm genuine.

She stays with me until a young resident doctor arrives. He's the one who'll decide whether or not I should be admitted.

He sits down facing me. He listens while I tell him that anxiety and suicidal thoughts the past several months have almost shredded me to nothing. I add that I have two children.

He looks at me. Then he says:

I had a bit of trouble making sense of the doctor's discharge file in connection with your stay at Frederiksberg Hospital.

I feel I'm being accepted into the community of humans.

I'm admitted to Bispebjerg Hospital. I curl up in my bed. I cry.

I don't dare tell Jan I've been hospitalized again.

I call Niels. I'm lying down on the bed with my mobile and speak softly. Niels says it's a good thing I've been admitted. I feel calmer. We talk about attachment patterns. Niels says he thinks Jan shows an insecure-dismissive attachment pattern and I an insecure-anxious attachment pattern.

They don't really go well together, I say.

Niels says he'll send a link to an article I could read.

A few hours later I send a long text message to Jan and tell him where I am. I write that I've become more aware of our divergent attachment styles and that I'm very much prepared to be better at dealing with his and not to talk about the two daily text messages anymore.

Emergency Room, Admission
Bispebjerg Hospital, Copenhagen
July 2016

During the night a tall, youngish man has arrived. Soky is his name. That's what he tells me.

A cool name, I say.

He rolls his eyes and says:

They just wanted it to be something special.

He has long blond hair and red fingernails. Several brightly coloured scarves tied around his neck. A face that's constantly at work. A brain that's always working overtime in an attempt to sort out everything in the world: television, cigarettes, networks, medicine, the United States' successive presidents, potential conspiracies in connection with 9/11, and the construction of the hospital's big new parkade. Never a moment of peace. I feel the urge to approach him, place my hands on his shoulders, look into his eyes, and whisper that not everything is that wild and violent, and we're not required to fully understand all the world's occurrences and their interconnections.

He walks over to the tea cart with the breakfast items. Puts a piece of cheese on a slice of bread and pours yogourt into a bowl. Brings it to the table. He takes a bite of the bread, puts it down, abandons the bread and the world, and slips into a whispery conversation with somebody I cannot see.

He's so thin, and I hope he'll soon feel sufficiently calm to take another bite, he probably can't feel his own body, his hunger, I'm thinking. But the nicotine urge is solid, he begins rolling a cigarette, his index and middle fingers are yellow next to the red nail polish. He rolls and licks and then seals the paper around the tobacco. Then he disappears to smoke outside.

The bread and the yogourt are still sitting there. He and John are deep in conversation about the parkade. The top floor is going to be used for some kind of landings, I overhear, the CIA is involved and several doctors at the hospital. John is standing with his arms hanging limp. Now and then Soky walks over to the corner of the terrace and moves his one arm up and down mechanically. It's something he's been told to do, I'm sure, by one of the voices. And there's no getting around it, he must obey or else the shit will hit the fan.

After two smokes he returns to the table and moves the cheese sandwich and the bowl with yogourt twenty centimetres to the left, first the bowl and then the sandwich. Meticulously. Now here they are. I don't know if it's the voices doing that too.

He gets talking with Elna. Earlier in the morning Elna had told me that on a sunny day she had felt like playing at being young and had sat down in the open window with her bare legs hanging outside, but then she had slipped—I was wearing a silk dress, she explains, those things are slippery—and she had fallen down two stories and broken her back.

Soky is telling Elna that the floors in his apartment at home have become porous, it began with a soft chewing sound that intensified as time passed, and then the floor planks became more and more shaved down, thinner and thinner, he could see it on the paths between the stacks of newspapers around the apartment. He only just managed to tear the oven door open, grab the melted plastic globe and get out of the apartment before the planks were shaved down to wood chips, and him falling through the floor.

Elna waits politely till he's finished, then tells him they are showing *Upstairs, Downstairs* again.

Soky takes a bite of his bread and cheese, it makes me happy, and I have a sudden impulse to lean across the table, distract him with something, and proceed to shovel the rest of the food into his mouth. But then John passes by with an unlit cigarette on his way to the smokers' terrace, and Soky reaches for his packet of Petterøe's tobacco and the rolling papers and follows him.

Late in the afternoon the consulting psychiatrist comes to my room. She tells me they would like to keep me for a while and that I'll be transferred to Frederiksberg Hospital.

I'm grateful.

We're considering the closed ward, she says.

I wouldn't like that, I say.

I'm scared I'll have to deal with the same doctor again, but I don't say it out loud.

There's a knock on the door, and Jan pokes his head in. He came back from Roskilde this morning.

I'll wait out here, he says, and sends me a smile.

Ward F3A
Frederiksberg Hospital, Copenhagen
July 2016

Jan and I bike from Bispebjerg to Frederiksberg Hospital. We walk up a stately staircase and into a wide, high-ceilinged hallway that leads to the open ward for affective disorders. We're received by an anemic nurse, her skin white and glossy and her voice so soft that I have to lean close to hear what she's saying. The spacious rooms and her politeness make me feel that we've entered a bygone era, that she's a maid and I a young lady having just arrived.

We're shown a sizable room down the hallway that reminds me more of a young woman's bedroom in a charitable institution from the beginning of the last century than a room in a psychiatric ward. In it are a bed, a wardrobe, an easy chair, a desk with a chair, and a whiteboard. At the end of the room is a large grid window facing a garden.

It's the psychiatric sensory garden, she says.

The place is bright and beautiful, and I can hardly believe my eyes.

I turn toward her.

I'm very grateful, I say, and not only for the nice room.

We sit down on the bed, Jan and I. I take a deep breath.

It'll be great, I say.

Yes, he says.

Here I think I'll be able to get help to recover, I say.

I think so too, he says.

He bends down and takes off his sneakers. Then he lies down on his back in the narrow bed and reaches for me. I place my thigh on top of him and rest my head against his chest. Stick my hand under his T-shirt and touch one of his nipples, which is a little hard dot. Under my thigh I can feel his dick, I'm aware of any movements in the institutional hallway out there. Aware of the nurse.

Sønder Vilstrup, Jutland
The 1970s

When Anne isn't at home, I get that pulling in my stomach. I'm restless. I'm being told to spit at regular intervals and count every step I take.

One of the barns is kept empty. Inside, a wet smell of mould. Rotten hay. Beams that are wasted away by dampness and caterpillars. There's a flattened, dried-up rat in the manure gutter. One, two, three, four, five, six, seven steps, and I'm past it. I like playing out here. Brick-built pigpens make up the rooms in my house. I sweep them and put out some wooden beer crates and tidy up while spitting. I'm scared of the rats but forget about them when I'm playing house. I pull strips of rotten wood from the large elm tree that fell over a long time ago behind the dung heap and bring it inside. It's my meat. I cook it in the blue pot with sand and dandelions.

I have three dolls. They sit in the pigpen. They are all called Karen, and the only thing I do with them is talk to them. I ask what they are, if they are dreamy and sensitive or strong and courageous. They answer in my voice while I look at them in turn and ponder which choice is the most desirable. I let them finish what they have to say until one of them goes down a path I don't like. She doesn't want to be either of the two choices, she wants to be mad and impossible, and I tell her that's not an option. There are only the two options I've just mentioned.

We also have three cats. They are not allowed inside the house. I think the cats are skinny. At Helle's they have a chubby cat that lies in their leather swivel chair. At Helle's they don't have any books, and in their bathroom a rope is fastened along the ceiling. Although it's utterly petit bourgeois, I think it's quite nice there. We're allowed to play with Barbie dolls. We sit with the dolls on the living room carpet. The radiators are turned on all winter.

When I'm at their place, I'm served cornflakes with whole milk and sugar. It's as if I cannot get enough, one portion after another disappears inside me.

I don't tell anyone what we're doing over at Helle's.

If one of our cats sneaks into the scullery to snatch a bite of Linka's food, my mother slides her foot under its belly and flings it out the door. The cat lands far from the door, screaming, and runs away.

I'm allowed to feed the cats because I have trouble falling asleep when I'm worried about them being hungry. I spread slices of rye bread with liver pâté, stack the slices, and cut them into small squares. I step out on the cobblestones by the scullery door and tip the squares into an old plate next to the propane tanks. Kitty, kitty, kitty, I call, and all of them come shooting out from the barns.

Sometimes I get tired. The chickens have to be tended to as well. They are kept in the yellow building. I tell my father you have to change their water every day. I don't know why I think that. He says you don't have to. Water is water. How can it be too old? I fish bits of hay out of the water trough. Occasionally I change the water too.

Later on Linka has puppies. It's unplanned. The pups are in one of the pigpens in the barn I play in. Linka looks at me when I climb over the wall into the pen. It lifts its tail a little but otherwise stays put with its suckling pups. I sit with them every day after school.

Out in the country it's like this: If there are any unwanted animals, you just kill them yourself. In the cities people are mushy, they call their animals "he" and "she." In the country we call them "it."

We're not keeping the pups.

My mother and father discuss at length how to kill them. Whether they should drown them. We don't like that, Anne and Niels and I. We try talking them out of it but don't know how you do those kinds of things.

They dismiss the idea of drowning them. It's better to gas them. Put them in a grain sack and tie it to the Volvo's exhaust pipe, they say. They'll do it next Saturday. During the days leading up to it, I spend as much time as possible in the pigpen with Linka and the pups.

Anne and Niels and I don't talk to each other about it. On the appointed Saturday we run upstairs to our rooms and lie on our beds with pillows covering our heads. But we can hear the car starting inside the barn. The engine is idling for a long time, maybe half an hour. Then it stops. But they don't come inside. Nothing happens for a long time.

Then we hear them in the scullery. We run downstairs. They look terrified, they are pacing back and forth, speaking fast.

The pups didn't die, my father says.

We're standing in the middle of the floor, staring at them. Niels with his fingers in his mouth. Anne's eyes look wild, I think she has been crying, I don't know where to go.

They say the pups were lying in a jumble on the bottom of the sack and looking up at them when they untied the sack from the exhaust pipe.

We had to bash their heads on the cement floor, my mother says. Several times.

We'll never do it again, she continues.

My father shakes his head.

Even though it's only in the cities that you don't kill your animals yourself.

I don't like being in the barn anymore. Instead I cross the big plowed field between our farm and the Screamers' farm. A band of high-voltage power lines runs the length of the field. They hum. There's a hollow farther out, you can't see it from where I am, but if I run in that direction it will appear. Water from a flood last fall has accumulated there, and now there are ice floes and snow. A big, empty Western landscape like those I've seen in black and white films. I settle down by the edge of the lake and begin baking cornbread from the snow. Build my house with footprints in the snow.

Darkness has fallen without me noticing it. Between it and the furrows a white fog has settled. It's calm, no wind. Only the high-voltage lines are talking. I stand up, my knees are wet. Something has scared the rooks by our farm far away. They fly high up, screaming, and circle the air before settling in one of the dead trees. Dampness hangs in my hair. I dawdle back toward the trees and the barn. Heavy from the humidity, my woollen mittens flap against my legs.

I've been assigned two care workers who take turns according to who is on duty: Ellen and Svend. Ellen shows me the board where the schedule is posted. Here are all the names of the patients too: LIV, GOLFI, EJNER, MARIE, JONAS, KAREN. Next to our name is our respective room number and the name of our care worker for the day.

Ellen asks if we could go down to my room and talk.

She sits in the easy chair beside the desk. I sit on the desk chair.

I want to learn how not to be so dependent on my boyfriend, I say. Not to think so intensely about whether or not he's there for me, whether or not he loves me.

Yes, Ellen says. When you're completely wrapped up in your boyfriend, there's no one at home at your place.

I jump up, move the desk, lift the marker, and write on the board:

WHEN I'M COMPLETELY WRAPPED UP IN MY BOYFRIEND,
THERE'S NO ONE AT HOME AT MY PLACE

Then you become an empty shell, she says. And then you won't be able to take care of yourself.

My system is running at full throttle and I need things spelled out in simple Ga-Jolisms, as we used to call those types of sentences that were printed on the Ga-Jol licorice boxes back when I attended the Danish Academy of Creative Writing.

Supper is at six o'clock. Ten minutes to six, people start walking back and forth in the hallway outside my room. I go into the dining room at three minutes past six. The others are already seated, eating, looking down at their plates. They don't talk with each other. I make the rounds, shake hands with everybody, also with the staff. The care workers eat by themselves at a table next to the patients'. Ellen is standing by the food counter, she asks what I would like to have and serves it to me. I sit down with the others. No one says anything. The care workers talk to each other and occasionally say something to us. But getting us to participate in a normal conversation is hopeless.

Opposite me is Liv. I think she's pretty. Her blond hair is tied up in an enormous bun on top of her head. She's looking down at her plate, her expression the most despondent I've seen in a long time.

As soon as we have finished eating—it takes maximum ten minutes—we leave the table, say thank you, scoop the leftovers, if any, into the garbage can, put the cutlery—here it's not plastic—in a metal tray with water, put the plate and the glass down beside it. We're meticulous and extremely well mannered.

At seven o'clock Jan arrives. I recognize his steps and run out to meet him.

Should I ask if we can go for a walk? I say. After all, it isn't very cheerful here.

I'm ashamed of being one of those you visit in a place like this.

I have to write my name on a board just inside the door and

add the time I expect to be back. We walk in our usual quick tempo to Frederiksberg Have, make the rounds in the park, and end up by the fountain next to Møsting's House and Café Svejk and the ice cream stand. We buy a coffee and sit down outside in a patch of sunlight.

Sønder Vilstrup, Jutland
1981

Anne enjoys high status in our family. She can put everybody in their place, even my father, should they act unreasonably toward each other. As, for instance, when I'm fourteen and suddenly start swelling up.

He's sitting in the easy chair, reading by one of the bookcases in the large living room. His big reading glasses sit halfway down his nose. Sensing that he's occupied with what he's doing, I step into the room without any concerns. My back is toward him so I don't notice the change of expression on his face until it's too late.

I can't stand looking at your big ass! he bellows.

I flinch. Also because of the sudden loud sound.

I turn toward him. His face is twisted with disgust. His mouth hangs slack. He looks me straight in the face.

I rush out. Stand in the middle of the dining room. There's a carpenter's plane with a steel blade that sits on his worktable out in the yellow barn and I want to pull it down over my body. Slice off my ass and breasts, fat, everything that has accumulated on my bones. The foreign layers that aren't me, the layers that have invaded me.

Anne has gone in to see him. He's still sitting in the chair. She looms large in front of him.

162

You don't say things like that, dammit! she shouts.

I'm standing on the same spot in the middle of the dining room. He gets up and walks into the room where I am. He's holding the reading glasses in his hand. He looks anguished.

I'm sorry, he says.

His eyes appear wild.

I can't look into them.

It's okay, I mumble.

I learn to move in a certain way so I always face him.

Psychoeducation is on the agenda at F3A, and we're going to talk about self-worth. It's not something any of us has had much of. It turns out, for instance, that we've all been bullied at school. We are Jonas and Marie and I. And Svend, one of my two care workers.

Jonas has a suckermouth. Large, fleshy lips in a soft, childlike face full of thick red stubble. He's twenty-nine, and this is his first hospital stay. The food on the ward is a *huge* problem for him. Rice goes with beef stroganoff and curried chicken. But they serve either boiled potatoes or instant mashed potatoes. So Jonas orders takeout delivered to F3A by Just Eat and sits down defiantly, bent over the white containers, while we silently eat beef stroganoff with instant mashed potatoes. A week later Jonas gets the idea that he can boil the rice himself in the kitchenette area in the living room. Eventually he manages to negotiate a deal, something to do with the Food Safety Agency, but the upshot of it is that Jonas shows up with his pot full of rice every evening.

Jonas has done his homework. He's worked, among other things, on the so-called "Personal Rights." Marie and I haven't started yet.

When he was home on the weekend, and his mother and sister had asked if he wanted to come along and get some type of takeout rice dish, he had replied:

I reserve my right to decline.

On the chart of "Personal Rights," it says among other things that we may reserve the right to decline.

Svend nods approvingly and says:

What did they say to that?

Jonas says:

They said, what the hell do you mean by that?

I hold my breath, and Jonas clicks his ballpoint pen, he always does that when he talks, and I'm constantly worried that somebody will ask him to stop because then he'll stop talking too. It's so important that we talk.

Svend doesn't say anything, he looks at Jonas, holding back.

I want to stick a soother in Jonas's mouth.

But Jonas comes back with more:

I said, it means I don't feel like coming along.

Svend nods and asks how they reacted to that.

They just said, oh, okay, Jonas says.

I breathe a sigh of relief and lean back in my chair.

Sønder Vilstrup, Jutland
and Provence, France
The 1980s

In our family a natural law prevails:

My mother and father and I cannot love each other at the same time. My father is certainly capable of loving me. But if he does, my mother is not able to love him or me. If she loves me, it generally doesn't have much to do with me, it's because we are ganging up on him and attacking him. And if my mother and father love each other, no one will love me.

The first time we drive south, my mother and father love each other.

I'm fourteen years old, and my mother and father and Niels and my grandmother and grandfather and I drive through Jutland in two cars. Our Volvo 544 and their orangey-yellow Ford Taunus. We're going to Provence, France, where we have borrowed an old town house in a small medieval town with its pale-yellow houses and plane trees situated on top of a hill surrounded by purple fields of fragrant lavender. Our annual vacations have up to now included hiking trips in Norway or Sweden and once in East Germany. It's considered lowbrow to go south and follow the flood of tourists on their package vacations.

But now we're taking the plunge. And I think it's also something we're doing for my sake. Twice a year we receive catalogues, one from Spies Vacations and one from Tjæreborg Travels. I settle down on the couch with the catalogues, and I can hardly wait to browse through the glossy pages and look at the small pictures of azure swimming pools, white hotels, happy people, white beaches, and green palm trees. I love the sun and the heat, and swimming, but have only done so in the North Sea and Limfjorden, in Swedish lakes, Norwegian rivers, and ice-cold mountain lakes. Splashing around in water that is warm strikes me as being absolutely fantastic. Not to mention jumping into a swimming pool.

I think my mother and father have been aware of this. For, in spite of Karen Blixen's stork, school ends up making me sick, and I have no idea how to make friends or avoid being teased. My stomach begins to burn toward the end of Grade 6. And it continues during the following year. In the beginning I bring biscuits to school, and milk, but eventually I bring pills that I have to chew slowly. The milk and the biscuits and the pills smother the acid bath in my stomach. But it quickly starts bubbling again, and after one year the acid has rasped away a spot in my innards, and I'm developing an ulcer.

I'm given permission to bike home from school. I cycle slowly and hunched over, one arm cradling my stomach. I usually manage the six kilometres from school pretty fast, but today it's taking a long time. I have to take breaks at regular intervals and lie down on the shoulder of the road. Once in while a car passes by, and the driver looks at me while I try flatten myself in the grass by the edge of the ditch so he won't see me. The picture of me lying there beside the bicycle with the front wheel still spinning is all wrong.

Finally I make it home, and I decide to phone my mother. She says she'll leave right away. My father comes home as well.

And then the three of us are actually there, together. For the first time. I lie down on the corner sofa in the large living room, and they sit on either side of me. I'm not good at relaxing and breathing slowly, even though they try showing me how to do it. Sometimes I'm close to screaming. But I'm incredibly happy. For my mother and father are with me, both of them, we're together, and they look afraid. They are afraid because *I'm* hurting. It makes me dizzy from happiness. And I nearly wish the pain will last forever.

They call the doctor several times. In the end they start arguing, I can no longer hear what they are saying, but I sense it's not because they are angry with each other, it's because they are scared. So I still feel calm. Later in the evening my father lifts me up and carries me out to the Volvo, and they put me in the back seat and wrap me in the duvet.

When we arrive at Fredericia Hospital, my father carries me again. At emergency he lays me down on a gurney, and I'm wheeled into a cubicle. A doctor and some nurses stand around me, lean over me, and I start feeling apprehensive.

I have to swallow a black tube, thick as a finger, with a camera at the end. They ask me to relax. But I start gagging when the tube is squeezed down my throat, and at the same time I'm afraid I can't breathe. They say I have to help them, I have to swallow it, perform the necessary muscular movements, otherwise the tube won't move along. I want to pull the tube out, but somebody is holding my arms. After I've swallowed the tube and it's all the way down in my stomach, it isn't so terrible anymore. They take pictures and observe that the inner lining is worn thin.

After the tube has been removed, my mother and father drive back home, and I'm being wheeled into a room where I have to sleep. Two old men and an old woman are in the room. They are sleeping. Breathing heavily, sighing and moaning and making choking sounds through their open mouths as if their tongues are too big and in the way. The lights are turned off. I stare into the darkness through my enormous eyes.

The next day I'm wheeled down to another examination room. The doctor presses his hand on my stomach. It hurts, and I'm about to cry. But I control myself and say that it doesn't hurt. It's as if the doctor and the nurse don't believe me.

Does it hurt here? they ask.

I shake my head.

Here?

No, I say, clenching my teeth.

They look at each other.

I want to go home, I say.

They give me permission to use the patients' telephone, I call my mother and father and say that I want to go home immediately. I'm not keen on being alone any place other than at home, and at my grandmother and grandfather's house. I'm such a crybaby.

My parents come to get me, and when I walk toward the car I try to walk like somebody who's fit and healthy for fear of somebody spying on me behind the windows, looking for signs of me being unwell. They might come out and catch me and bring me back to the old people with the big tongues.

A couple of weeks later we're on our way to Provence, the promised South with its warm water. I've got my nose in a book. My father indicates that I ought to look at the landscape around us, but I keep on slipping back to the book.

Down through Germany it gets warmer and warmer, and my grandfather is about to boil over. Heat like this is beyond anything he's ever imagined. He's never been south of the Danish border. All he can think of is a glass of cold, fizzy beer. He talks about that beer. He twists and turns in the back seat with his cane squeezed tight between his pale thighs. He doesn't want water. His body is moving restlessly, longing for this large, cold glass of beer. I'm sitting beside him, and I look up to see his face. It's hard to understand why he can't just drink from our bottle with the lukewarm water. But I realize that something profound is at work here, something I cannot fathom.

And when we eventually park in the square in Heidelberg and sit down around a circular café table and order the enormous beer for my grandfather, we all stare at this broad, strong man while he takes long, greedy gulps of his beer and afterwards slumps blissfully back in his chair and finally becomes himself again. He winks at me and Niels, tickles us, talks about how incredibly beautiful it is here.

Look at the mountains out there!

His eyes fill with tears at the thought of it.

They are blue, he says.

The following day we cross the border between Germany and Switzerland. We're being stopped by the border patrol officers who want to know what we have brought with us, and they ask my father to open the trunk so they can see what's inside.

My grandfather, who's sitting in the back seat, sweating, says:

Lemme outta here!

And we jump up and push the back of the front seat down so he can drag himself out with his cane and wooden clogs. He walks around to where the Swiss customs officers stand and pulls one thing after another out of the trunk and shoves them into the men's faces:

Here is a pitcher and a sock, he says in his regional dialect.

The officers stand back. They look confused.

And here's a piss-pot, he says, and waves his chamber pot in front of the two young men.

We're given permission to continue our travels.

There's a certain dryness in the landscape and the town we're staying in, something I've never experienced before. Even the smells seem dry. And when I slide my fingers across the surface of the walls outside, white dust settles in the lines on my fingertips. The sun feels like pinpricks on my skin, and I change colour.

How pretty Karen looks, my father says affectionately. Your eyelids are tanned.

I hurry inside to see myself in the mirror as soon as we're back at the house. My father observes and observes, even the smallest things.

Although he says these things to me, my mother doesn't get miffed at him nor distance herself from him. I've never seen them this way. They are silly, fool around, and laugh and hold hands when out walking. It feels as if they aren't grown-ups any longer, and Niels and I think it's very awkward being in their company. We feel that we are the grown-ups in spite of us being eleven and fourteen and Niels only a sliver of a boy with white hair.

In the evenings, especially, something dark grows inside me. It begins before I go to bed but gets worse once I'm lying down. I feel as if there's a hole inside me. I don't know who I am. It's you, Karen, I say sometimes when standing in front of the mirror. I can see the image over there in the mirror, but the spot where I should be standing seems empty.

In bed in the evening it's hard feeling that hollow. I want to reach out and grab something to hold on to. Or I wish that something would reach out to me and hold me fast. Every morning

I'm unspeakably ugly because I fall asleep with weepy-puffy eyes, and it only gets worse as the night proceeds. I'm ashamed of my puffy eyes, but no one ever calls attention to them. Not even my grandmother with her large eyes behind her magnifying eyeglasses.

The day before our one and only excursion to the warm water in the Mediterranean, I pluck up courage and write a letter. I write:

Dear Mom,
 I'm sad, I feel lonely, and I miss you.
 Love from Karen

I sneak upstairs and put it under her pillow.

The next morning my eyes aren't puffed up. I look expectantly at my mother when she enters the living room. She sits down at the table, pours the coffee, and talks with my father.

I don't know what I expected. But probably that something or other would happen.

Off we go. With bathing suits and towels and coffee in the thermos. An hour and a half later we park the two cars—yes, I can hardly believe my eyes—under palm trees. It's a very impressive town we've arrived at. The pavement is in good shape, with fine white stripes, no holes. The houses are white and pretty, and the people walking around are nice-looking, they wear sunglasses on top of their heads. They seem relaxed and at home in this impressive place, while we feel a little uneasy. My father looks troubled.

It's also because I have my period and I'm not about to miss a swim in the warm water, so he'll try to rent one of the beautiful beach cabins where I'll be able to leave my blood-red menstruation pad on the bench inside.

It works out for us, all of it, and we manage to get into the water. It's wonderful. And when I stand out there in the warm water, I can see mountains and palm trees and white houses. It's the most beautiful thing I've ever seen. But we're not staying here for long. We're strangers here, we have to get back quickly.

I'm thinking that perhaps my mother didn't find my letter. So when we arrive at the house, I sneak upstairs and lift her pillow to see if it's still there.

It isn't.

Ward F3A
Frederiksberg Hospital, Copenhagen
July 2016

Petting in hospital beds in psychiatric wards is unsatisfactory, so we go over to my apartment. We say we're going for a walk in Frederiksberg Have.

Jan is lying on his back, and I lick his lips. I bite his chin, and he smiles, but I'm not doing it for fun, I need to grasp him, feel his cartilage and tissue and skin and flesh with my teeth. I bury my face in his armpit and breathe in his odour. He doesn't laugh at that anymore. I'm an animal. I take his dick in my mouth, and he lifts himself up to look at me and says it looks sexy, beautiful, my lips and fingers around his dick.

My little sweetie, he says.

I'm lying on my back, and he strokes my pubis and says that my pussy is so delicate, so beautiful, and my breasts the most exquisite he's ever seen. When I sit on his dick, and he takes hold of my hips, his tone of voice is different. Then he says:

Now, come!

As if he knows that he can dictate my orgasm. And the fact that he's thinking this makes me come a few seconds after. Which he does too, we always come crashing at the same time.

The following evening he picks me up at F3A, and we walk about in Frederiksberg Have, talking about this and that. When we arrive at Café Svejk, he doesn't order coffee. He orders beer. It surprises me. He doesn't care much for alcohol.

We sit down in the evening sun on the sidewalk by Smallegade. Then he says:

I want to leave you now.

Jan could have said:

I'm going to have a sex reassignment surgery.

It would have caught me equally off guard. I want to scream. There's no room for me in my body.

I stand up and sit down again.

I say:

Yesterday you said that my pussy was delicate.

I notice his neck and face turning red.

Then he says:

I need a lot of alone time, as you know. But on the days when we aren't together, I'm worried about you. And the result is that on those days I'm not able to recharge. And then I don't get anything out of my alone time.

I say:

There's so much love between us.

He doesn't say anything.

I continue:

A month ago you gave me a ring as a present and said that now we had reached the point where earrings and necklaces weren't the only things you wanted to give me.

He looks at me, and I can tell there's something that's hurting him.

I say:

You promised me that you would never leave me from one day to the next without warning. Without giving me a chance to correct things.

Yes, he says, that's true. But you *keep on* being sick.

I notice the emphatic *keep on*.

No! I say. I'm going to get well.

He accompanies me back to F3A. We stand in the hallway just inside the door.

I love you so much, I say.

I know, he says.

I ask if I may have a final hug. I may.

I take off my jacket.

So that I can feel it better, I say.

After which he leaves.

I start running around, up and down the hallway, into the day room. I call Svend. Doors are opening. Jonas comes out.

Where is Svend? I yell at him.

Jonas looks frightened.

Down there, I think, he says.

I continue running, bumping into things, I'm running much too fast.

Svend comes out from one of the other rooms.

What happened? he says.

He accompanies me down to my own room, closes the door behind us. I'm pacing back and forth. He grabs hold of me, pulls me in close, holds me tight for a long time, and I calm down a bit.

I say:

You'll have to give me something strong now.

He nods.

It's okay, he says.

He leaves to get some benzodiazepines while I'm stomping around the room.

This thing, Svend says, when he returns, this thing has nothing to do with you.

I don't know what it means, I want the benzodiazepines. I take them, and Svend helps me get into bed. He sits down in the chair beside me.

I doubt everything now. My world is without any fundamental laws.

I call Niels.

Jan has left me, I say.

I'm not surprised, Niels says. I feared it would happen once you were hospitalized.

PART

FOUR

Ward F3A
Frederiksberg Hospital, Copenhagen
July 2016

It's Friday, and everyone is leaving for the weekend. I'm the only one not allowed to go home.

I'm in my room when I hear Ida's footsteps, she walks fast.

She hugs me, looks serious, squeezes me. My anxiety lets up for a moment. We sit on my bed, holding hands.

Should we go and sit in that garden down there? she says.

The psychiatric sensory garden? I say.

Yes, she says, I couldn't remember what it's called.

Because the closed ward is using the garden right now, the iron gates, several metres tall, are shut and locked, and you can neither enter nor exit it. We wait until they are gone and the gates have been opened.

Subsequently we walk in and sit down on the grass. The sun is shining, it's warm. Ida is able to draw anxiety out of bodies. She looks me in the eyes incessantly. Stares into them until something ruptures and my fear begins to seep out. After which blissful seconds or perhaps even minutes pass without anxiety. Until it starts building up again in there.

Ida is in the middle of getting a divorce. The Ga-Jolism that says when you're completely wrapped up in your boyfriend, there's no one at home at your place, makes sense in her case too, she says. So we make a pact on the lawn in the psychiatric sensory garden. The pact has two items:

1) We don't want to be dependent on men.
2) We don't want a boyfriend until we're completely self-reliant and have taken control of our lives.

We make yet another plan: we'll get me out for the night and go over to my apartment and sleep there.

At eight thirty we get up to walk back to F3A. But without our noticing it, the tall gates have now been closed shut and locked. The thought of us having to spend the night locked inside a psychiatric sensory garden makes us laugh.

We shout in the direction of the windows.

There's someone up there, isn't there? I say.

Yes, Ida says.

She can shout very loudly.

Hey! she shouts. You, up there!

Finally someone opens a window, and a man pokes his head out and asks where we belong.

F3A, I shout. We've been locked in.

He comes downstairs and lets us out.

When we're back at F3A, I say to the polite nurse, the one with glossy white skin, that we want to sleep at home, at my place.

I'm sneaky and choose to formulate it like this:

I'm afraid of having to sleep alone tonight here. It'll result in my spending the night twisting and turning and feeling anxious. Therefore I really, really want to sleep with Ida. At home in my own apartment.

The nurse looks doubtful. Looks at each of us in turn. I'm her responsibility.

I've known Ida for almost thirty years, I say. She's my best friend. You can trust her to take care of me.

There's a pause in the exchange. Then she looks at Ida, seriously. We try to look grown-up and responsible.

You'll have to promise me not to leave Karen by herself! she says.

Yes, of course, I promise, Ida says.

Thank you, I say, and we start packing up a few things in a hurry as if we were preparing an escape.

When we lie in bed in my apartment, we modify the pact.

Ida? I say. We're allowed to have lovers, aren't we?

Yes, yes, of course, she says. That's a whole different story!

I rarely hear Liv speak. She seems immersed in what patients with deep depressions are stuck in. I never talk to her. I think she's too far gone. She sits across from me in the dining room, her back straight and the big blond bun on her head. She looks down at her food.

But today she suddenly says something to me.

She lifts her eyes, looks at me, and says:

I'm sorry your boyfriend has left you.

Her face expresses empathy.

I'm very surprised. I truly didn't think she was aware of her surroundings.

Thank you for saying that, I say. It's very sweet of you.

She looks at her food again. With her back straight, her head lowered.

Golfi told me, she says.

Golfi likes to stay close to me, and therefore she knows everything because she observes everything. She sees me cry, sees me stare into space, sees me working out like a lunatic.

Did he take off just like that? Liv says. He was here quite a lot though.

I'm thinking that it's too bad I've misjudged Liv's condition. I could have had other people to talk to besides Golfi and Marie during my stay here. The problem might also be due to the fact that I'm the only non-smoker on the ward, and many of the conversations take place downstairs around the smokers' table in the parking lot. I'm missing out on those.

We both get up from our chairs. We scrape the leftovers into the garbage can and put the plates and cutlery away with great care. Liv is going downstairs to smoke, I'm going to sit on the couch in the hallway and stare into space.

Then the alarm goes off. It happens about once a day. It can be heard all over the ward, long, loud beeping sounds, while a red sign on the large display above the hallway flashes on and off.

It spells POLICE.

The entire staff is running, they disappear immediately, and we're left alone. We feel somewhat ill at ease like when Mom and Dad go out.

Golfi stands by the window and looks down at the parking lot by the closed ward.

What's happening? I ask Golfi.

There's trouble in the closed ward, she says, her eyes wide open.

They've called the police, but the staff also has to be present down there when there's a problem, she explains.

I'm still a novice.

I press my forehead against the window to get a better look.

They can go completely berserk down there, she says, looking at me with dilated pupils.

The others have arrived too, we're all clustered around the window. A police car drives into the lot. There's quite a commotion down there. A little later an ambulance arrives, and twenty minutes later we see the paramedics wheeling out a person on a gurney.

The following day Golfi tells me that the person died. She can ferret out anything. I don't know how she does it. Surely she can't communicate with the folks in the closed ward. I've been there so I know you can barely push the windows open more than ten centimetres. But I believe her. She knows her shit.

Ward F3A
Frederiksberg Hospital, Copenhagen
July 2016

Today I'm going down to join the smokers. Golfi and Liv are there. Golfi is talking. She's talking about a dog. Someone has beaten it to a pulp, and there's a screaming guy at the Sankt Hans Psychiatric Centre, Ejner has told her.

We held a farewell party for Ejner the other night. Liv had decorated with balloons, and we sang for him.

We sing every morning too.

One, two, three, Svend says.

And then we get going, each in their own key.

After a three-month waiting period, Ejner has finally been transferred to Sankt Hans to join other patients with dual diagnosis, addicts with mental illness. But he took off after two days, and now he's back at the Oasis of Everyday Life, his regular pub.

He has no doubt dropped his Antabuse, says Golfi, jeeeeez, and if this annoying guy yells at me, she continues, I'll bloody well hammer him one.

Golfi has also been assured of a place at Sankt Hans.

But jeeeeez, that dog, really! she says, rolling her eyes. Beaten to a pulp.

Golfi can talk non-stop, in a series of three or four loops that go round and round, each time with the exact same measured intonation. Sometimes her voice *can* sound uncertain, as when she rattles on about the screaming guy, but usually it sounds monotone with deep back vowels typical of the Vesterbro district. And she will go on and on telling one horrible story after another, her head tilted back, her eyes darting from side to side.

Her anxiety flutters in the space between us. I don't have the energy to do anything about it. And besides, I sense that Golfi operates under different rules than me. Her anxiety is not to be seen. So we have to pretend it isn't there.

It's that screaming guy, she repeats.

Liv turns toward me as if she wants to say something.

But Golfi carries on. Now she's talking about Marie, who arrived at F3A in the middle of a manic episode. She had invested in seventeen outfits at the Umbrella, a drop-in centre for the mentally ill and other vulnerable people on Nyelandsvej, close to the hospital. Naturally everyone had hoped that especially a place like that would be understanding and take back at least sixteen of the outfits.

And there were flowers everywhere, Golfi says.

Liv looks down at her lap.

Marie stuck them in here and there, Golfi continues. Into the electric kettle in the dayroom. And the ashtray was full of them, like it was a fucking flowerpot.

She nods in the direction of the large cement ashtray.

It was impossible to butt out your smoke, for crissakes.

And the boxes with rat poison, Liv says quietly.

Golfi opens her eyes wide.

Yes, she stuffed flowers into both ends, like they were over-flowing.

It was actually beautiful, Liv says.

Golfi looks uncertain, as if she can feel that Liv needs some space too. I'm wondering if that's how she functions: talking keeps anxiety at bay.

I don't know how intense her anxiety is right now, in any case she keeps quiet.

Liv straightens up and looks me firmly in the eye.

I'm so ashamed of my diagnosis that I can't even tell people what it is, she says.

There are tears in her eyes.

I say:

Then you probably have the same as me. Borderline personality disorder.

You have that too? she says.

Yes.

She looks devastated.

I say:

I've felt the same way, but lately not so much.

Liv frowns.

No? she says.

I watched a lecture about BPD on YouTube, I say. The psychologist said we have more zip. While other people are more like Germans, we are like the Spanish people.

I smile at her.

Being Spanish isn't the most boring thing, is it? I say. Like black-haired and passionate.

Sønder Vilstrup, Jutland
The 1980s

We're hiding two rejected Iranian refugees at the time I'm attending high school. We appeal their case, and they end up being granted asylum. Meanwhile I teach them Danish. And fall in love with them. I'm a steaming kettle. My parents keep an eye on me.

We sit by the dining table and work on Danish grammar. My mother sits at the other end of the room reading the daily *Kolding Folkeblad*. Then Reza asks me:

Where's nice dot on girl?

Kolding Folkeblad ceases to rustle. I don't understand what he means.

What nice dot?

He tilts his head back, sticks his tongue out, and shakes his head.

Like this, he says.

And now I'm getting an idea of what he means.

I turn the paper over where I've written a list of verbs and begin to draw a woman's body.

Reza and Masoud pay careful attention. Then I grab a red pen.

Here, naturally, I say, putting a dot between her legs while working hard at appearing completely relaxed.

Kolding Folkeblad is far too quiet.

And here.

I put a dot on each breast.

And here too, I say, adding dots to the neck, the mouth, the ears, the armpits, the stomach, the inner thighs.

Before too long the drawing looks like a girl with German measles.

Okay, of course it differs a bit from girl to girl, I explain.

We're two families in my family: We're a patriarchal, puritan family from long before the youth rebellion and sexual revolution. And we're a liberated, progressive family from after the advent of the youth rebellion and sexual revolution. I can tell that my parents, especially my father, are sometimes close to being torn in half. His face begins to twitch, tics appear around his eyes, and then all sorts of devilry sputters from his mouth. It's the puritan patriarch who boils over when the modern era, which he prefers to see himself as being part of, becomes unbearable. And when those things, which his own liberal, progressive persona has put in motion, become intolerable to him.

It's also difficult for us, his daughters, to strike a balance in that fissure between the two poles. We join him at Kolding Højskole, where wearing bras and bikini tops would be considered a sign of oppression against women and fear of the naked body, basic principles created by the founding members, including my father.

But suddenly the puritan devil possesses him, and disgust runs down his face while he spews out words:

Go inside and put on a shirt. I can't swallow my food if I have to look at your breasts!

The explosions usually come without warning and frighten me to the point where I can sense the fear around my rectal muscles; I'm afraid my bowels will begin to empty while I sit in the lawn chair.

I turn scarlet and wish I could get rid of my body. Just have a skeleton coated with skin. Or not have a body at all.

Wrapping it up and putting it away is not a possibility. It would collide with the other family we are. And it wouldn't work anyway because I have little else in my head other than thoughts about sex and my body. But also because a demon has possessed *me*: has turned me into a wild rebel. I've become impossible.

Niels has found an old VéloSoleX moped somewhere that Reza and Masoud have begun to fix out in the barn. They want to give it to me. I follow their work intently—if they can get it going, it'll be easier for me to get out of here. As things stand now, as in the past, I have my bicycle and the bus, and the bus stop is one and a half kilometres from where we live, and the last departure from Kolding (fifteen kilometres from home) is at 6:35 p.m. every day. Fridays and Saturdays included.

After having worked on the VéloSoleX for about a week, they finally manage to get it started. We fill it up with gas, and images of myself driving away in the dark, in case I need to get away, pop into my head. I kiss Reza and Masoud on the cheek.

In the evening I mount the rusty machine to drive the ten kilometres down to see my high school friend Casper, who lives in Skærbæk. It's going tremendously, and I feel free. But after four kilometres the moped starts sputtering fire. It gushes from the engine that sits on the front fork, and I jump off and toss it to the ground, afraid it might suddenly explode.

I was driving in a cone of light with the choppy engine sound in my ears. Now it's completely dark, and silent. Black tree trunks surround me. An owl sets off with its heavy wings and its hoot. I look around, my eyes adjusting to the darkness. There's nothing else I can do but walk home. I'm down in a hollow with dense forest all around. But soon I'm further up, which is almost worse. For here there's nothing but plowed fields and a strong wind shaking the naked trees. I can choose either to follow the road or walk across the fields and cut my hike short a kilometre. I choose the fields. It's heavy walking in the clay dirt. Lumps are forming under my boots. I squeeze through the hedgerows that form the boundaries between the fields. There are a few farmhouses here and there. And clouds sweeping across the moon.

In the beginning I cry, but eventually I start shouting into the wind:

Dammit! Shit! What the hell! What the fuck am I supposed to do now?!

During those years I'm more confused than normal, and my parents do what they can to navigate through it.

For instance, one day a small Fiat is driving up the gravel road. We can see it from the dining room. Very few cars come our way, so we always look up when we hear an engine. We know the cars that drive on the dirt road Kæret. We don't recognize this one. It drives slowly, hesitantly, and comes to a crawl at our driveway. We hear it shortly after on the gravel in the farmyard.

My mother is out in the kitchen.

It stopped here, she says.

Before I can make it to the kitchen, she continues, incredulous: There are two black-haired men inside it.

Now I can see the car from the kitchen window, but I don't understand what I see.

Mom, I say, they live in Naples!

In Naples! she bursts out.

I nod without taking my eyes off the small car and the two black-haired men who are getting out and look totally out of place in our yard.

Did you know anything about this? she asks.

I shake my head.

You'll have to go out and open the front door, she says.

I walk through the dining room, continue through the wide hallway, open the front door, and step onto the stoop.

Ciao, Carin! they say, and open their arms wide.

The only thing I feel like doing right now is folding up the two handsome men and stuffing them back into the Fiat. But instead I say:

Have you come from Naples?

Yes, they say, and smile. Long trippe.

I nod and visualize Niels's map of Europe.

In our family you don't bring guests to your room. Having visitors is a collective affair, and hence we drink tea together, all of us, around the dining table. Half or whole hours pass by awkwardly while our friends are questioned about literature, politics, and music. But today I'm grateful and thank god they are communists so my father can take over and talk politics with them while I stand still in the kitchen with my mother.

Why are they here? she asks.

I open my eyes wide.

I don't know, I say.

But, Karen? she says.

Okay, I kissed one of them behind a bush in Toulouse, I whisper.

I've just turned seventeen and was riding the Interrail in France earlier in the summer.

But I haven't told them they could come here. I didn't know they were coming.

She sighs. My father is struggling in there. Their English is not very good. They are talking about working conditions for factory workers in southern Italy.

What shall I do? I say, feeling despair rise inside.

My mother sighs. Reaches for a Red Look cigarette.

Accompany them to the campground in Kolding, she says, and show them around town for one day, and that's it.

Is that acceptable?

Yes, she says.

I let out a sigh of relief.

But one evening, when one of Denmark's leading jazz trumpet players visits us, is almost worse. As often happens during this period, it sort of comes tumbling out of the blue. I drift aimlessly around, following my body and impulses like a ship whose captain is dead drunk at the helm.

We're at Don Quixote in Kolding, my girlfriend and I. Kenny Drew and the Radio Big Band are playing, and I fall head-over-heels in love with the trumpet soloist like I pretty much do with all boys or men who can play music. It looks so awesome when he stands up and plays his solos. So powerful, it seems to me, and my body grows warm and buttery soft.

After the concert I hang out in the bar. And then it happens, the thing I haven't dared to wish for in my wildest dreams. The trumpet player walks over to me. He's quite a bit older than I am. He is cute, I like him. I'm sitting on a bar stool, he's standing beside me. I can't fathom how this is even possible. Not only is he a jazz musician, he is also from Copenhagen, it can't get much bigger than that. I'm full of laughter and warm, glowing feelings, and I tip my head back when he sticks his fingers in my short, nuclear-red hair. And when he takes my hand, I go happily with him across the street to Hotel Saxildhus.

There are green wall-to-wall carpets everywhere. It's dark and smoky. Pictures of Koldinghus Castle on the walls. Porcelain plaques. Poinsettias in the windows. The receptionist looks at me, and I feel as if I'm doing something improper. Suddenly I don't know who I am and what I want. Or if what I want or don't want is wrong. The trumpet player takes my hand again after he gets the key from the heavy brass panel. He strokes my forehead and my hair. I sense that he likes me, but I don't know anything.

The next morning I go directly to school from the hotel. I don't have a school bag and I'm wearing the same leopard-print party outfit from the previous night. I whisper to my friend Casper during social studies class.

Do you know what I did last night? I whisper.

No? he whispers.

I tell him, and he begins drawing trumpet-playing babies.

A month later I bump into the trumpet player again at the library in Kolding where I often go after school. He has a gig in town. I can tell he's happy to see me, but I get scared. During that period I live in a rented room in Kolding, and I could bring him there or we could go to Hotel Saxildhus. Or I could say no, thank you. But suddenly I spot my father, who's leaning over the albums in the jazz section, and I just want to be a little girl standing close to him.

There are no clear thoughts in my head. Only one impulse: to be with my mother and father. So, the result is that the jazz trumpet player comes along with us in the Volvo the entire fifteen kilometres past the plowed fields to Sønder Vilstrup. And once again my father does all he can to save the day. He even suggests that they play something.

My body is all tense. I feel sorry for my father, who's struggling at the grand piano, tied to the written notes while the trumpet player has his eyes closed, is relaxed and off in his own music, and we, my father and I, are feeling stressed and far too present, outside our bodies.

My father is trembling nervously, he knows the trumpet player of name, of course, being the jazz lover he is. And late in the evening, when I drag the trumpet player up with me to my old room with the pink walls, my father runs after me and demands I come downstairs to the living room.

It's the old patriarch who speaks:

The trumpet player need not feel obliged to sleep with the daughter of the house. As a token of his gratitude!

Everything crashes inside me. I feel cheap. A whore. And I'm even less sure of what I want for myself. At the same time I'm not entirely convinced that my father is right about the trumpet player only wanting to sleep with me because he feels obliged.

It's the rebel who replies:

Mind your own business!

But I'm full of shame.

Ward F3A
Frederiksberg Hospital, Copenhagen
July 2016

When Golfi is alone with me, she speaks differently. She doesn't swear, and she no longer calls the Psychiatric Centre in Roskilde by its old name, Sankt Hans, but calls it Roskilde. So it's Roskilde she's heading for. She hangs around my door, we're a kind of sisterhood attending the same things here on the psychiatric ward.

Mindfulness, for instance, which we attend in the ward's fitness room. We're allowed to be there alone, which I often am. I work out down there. But we have to set out the doorstop so the door won't close completely. The staff have to be able to see if somebody should suddenly have a panic attack or otherwise flip out.

But at the mindfulness sessions we're with Svend. We lie down on mats in a circle around him, and he turns on the tape recorder. We do mental body scans of our entire bodies, I switch to a different mode whenever the body is involved or when I exercise or practise relaxation, it feels good being in my body. But it's hard for the others, I can tell. And Golfi can barely manage, I'm too damned restless, she says, raising her trembling hand. Most of the patients on the ward can't do it at all and rarely attend the sessions when they have to do with the body, it hurts too much.

We also have to visualize our thoughts and emotions, see them as tree trunks floating in a river. To register their presence but let them float by without paying further attention to them. Just imagine being able to do that, I think. Being something *else*. Being able to protect your boundaries. And push all that—which I later learn is called hypermentalizing—out of your head and just sit and stare at the whole menagerie floating by in the river.

Svend comes into my room every morning.

Your system has gone wonky, Karen, he says.

I jump up, push the table off to the side, and write it on the whiteboard, in capital letters:

YOUR SYSTEM HAS GONE WONKY, KAREN

It remains there during my entire three and a half weeks of hospitalization in F3A.

It's mostly due to my anxiety. It's eating me up. It pulls and tears in my stomach as if a creature is sitting in there in the cold fog, eating me from the inside.

The world is not dangerous, Svend says, it hasn't changed. Only Jan isn't here any longer. Otherwise the world is as it used to be.

I devour everything he says, he is the hand that reaches across the abyss. I'm hanging on.

But you're thrown straight back to when you were very small and felt abandoned. It was dangerous then, and it made sense to be afraid. Today there's no danger. You're more than capable of taking care of yourself now.

Frederiksberg Neighbourhood in Copenhagen
August 2016

In August I'm being discharged. But a type of psychosocial plan of action has been devised to integrate me back into society. Twice a week Cognitive Johnny pays me a home visit. He walks slowly up the stairs to my apartment on the fifth floor, wearing his backpack. He puts it down on a chair by the dining table, unzips it, and pulls out cognitive charts.

Cognitive therapy is unsexy. It doesn't have the intellectual pizzazz of psychoanalysis. And I doubt I would have gotten as much out of it had it not been for the psychoanalytic therapy I received when young, dissecting my body that was eight months old, eighteen months, five years, fourteen, seventeen. Having picked the flesh off the bones. Seen how the body parts were connected, discovered how displaced they were. A leg sticking out of my back, a breast jiggling from my knee, a tongue sitting in my armpit.

But where I am now, it's fucking effective. And I submit to it, I'm all in.

Cognitive Johnny digs out three markers from his backpack: a green, a yellow, and an orange. Each of the week's events has to be marked with a colour. The green is for feeling good, the yellow for so-so, the orange for not so good.

You're filling your week up with too much, he says.

I see, I say.

What about your anxiety? he says. You should have marked those periods when you feel anxious in red, but apparently you have forgotten?

It's because I feel it all the time, I say, and look at him. So I thought it would be better not to cover the whole thing in red?

He remains silent for a while. Then he says:

It's okay.

Cognitive Johnny bends over his backpack again. This time he produces a chart. It's called "Cognitive Restructuring."

Do you want a ginger lozenge? he says, handing me the box.

I take one.

Thank you, I say.

Aren't they good? he says.

Yes, I say.

You can buy them in health food shops, he says.

I have to fill in the blank where it says: THOUGHTS. *What goes through your head?*

I bend over the table and write: When I'm alone in the evening, I think I don't belong to humanity. I'm not worthy of being part of the greater community.

The next rubric has the heading: PROOFS AND CONVICTIONS. *What is the proof of it being true? How convinced are you that it is true? 0%–100%*

I write: The proof is that I haven't been social for a long time. I'm 100% convinced.

The next rubric says: EMOTIONS. *What do you feel? How strong is the feeling? 0–10.*

I mull it over, then write: Anxiety 7. Feeling of loneliness 7–8.

The penultimate rubric says: ALTERNATIVE THOUGHTS. COUNTER-ARGUMENTS. *What should you focus on to make it better? Find new arguments that will alter your thinking.*

I write: Many people want to see me—I'm the one who has gone into isolation.

The last rubric says: EMOTIONS. *Have your feelings changed? How strong are they now? 0–10.*

I write: My anxiety is reduced to 2. The feeling of loneliness is 2.

Cognitive Johnny leans back.

Good, he says, and pushes the box with ginger lozenges in my direction.

I look at him.

Yes, sure, I say. It's working *now*. But I can guarantee you that tonight it won't.

He gathers up his markers and puts them in his backpack.

Maybe not tonight, he says. But if we carry on with it, it will eventually work.

We'll carry on, I say.

Good, he says.

I still miss Jan terribly, I say.

He zips up the backpack and looks at me:

When I was seventeen I suffered terrible heartaches. Then my father would say to me: There'll always be another girl and a streetcar too.

I think it's an idiotic thing to say. Throwing an old, tired song on the table. But I smile politely.

Frederiksberg Neighbourhood in Copenhagen
August 2016

Frederiksberg municipality gives me not only Cognitive Johnny but also Mentor Iben. She arrives on her bicycle once a week and shows up in the stairwell outside my door with nice red cheeks and a cheerful smile.

I'm on sickness leave and receive public assistance for three months, and Mentor Iben is going to help me with understanding and replying to the inquiries from the authorities and with navigating through an economy that has capsized after more than one year of me being sick.

She's nattering and chuckling, and I'm sitting beside her rigid as a shell. But make no mistake: Mentor Iben is crafty. She knows all about municipal offices and the tax department, about budgets and Mybanker.dk, and she is just pretending we're two girlfriends having a nice chat and a cup of coffee while taking care of five phone calls to the authorities and cancelling payments on online banking and setting up budgets.

The fact is that her project is not only trying to bring order to my finances, but also, like F3A, Ida, Anne, and Cognitive Johnny, to stir up a sense of self-worth in a shaky shanty town.

I observe everything from the outside, from the outer surface of my empty frame.

Should I write an email to the tax department? I say mechanically.

Shouldn't we just phone them right now? she says, and moves closer to me.

Yes, I say, and I feel my pulse pounding like crazy in the carotid artery.

Mentor Iben pushes the cellphone toward me and recites the numbers I have to key in, as if we are still two friends on equal footing. One digit at a time, very slowly.

We're on speaker phone, and she makes all sorts of grimaces as if she thinks it's party time, all the while whispering:

Ask them if you can get an installment plan now or if it has to go to debt collections.

My armpits are wet, and I feel the drops running down my side.

Hey, you managed that easily, she says, as if I'm a hell of a guy.

Frederiksberg Neighbourhood in Copenhagen
September 2016

My hands are shaking when I install Tinder on my cellphone.

Ida and I have made our pact, but I could do with some sex and a pair of eyes to look into. I want a lover. Lovers are permitted, according to the slightly revised pact. We talk quite a bit about the ways boyfriends differ from lovers. It has something to do with the idea that lovers aren't introduced to your siblings and definitely not to your children. That they come and go with higher frequency. That you may have several at the same time. That you don't develop any kind of dependency on them.

Niels has told me that people are using Tinder now. Our age group as well. I sit on the floor cross-legged, my back straight and tense, and select pictures of myself and write a very long profile.

Then I get going.

I swipe. One face after another, half-naked, posing bodies, gazing heavily as if we're already in the process of screwing, huge numbers of pictures of men on mountain bikes, or running, in fitness centres with puffed-up biceps and chest muscles. I swipe and swipe and gawk and gawk. They don't write very much, I discover. No doubt I've written far too much. Many of the same comments appear:

I'm inked, and so are you! I'm a non-smoker, and so are you! I'm fit, and so are you! I have the children on alternate weeks, and so have you!

I swipe exclamation marks and commands to the left.

Suddenly I see a young, incredibly beautiful man with a black beard and long black hair. He is seventeen years younger than me, a graduate student working on his thesis.

I don't give a shit, I whisper, I'm going to swipe to the right! My phone dings. It startles me.

Then our faces slide toward each other on the screen, and the word *Match* appears.

I spring to my feet.

What?! I say.

I walk a few rounds on the floor. Then I sit down again.

I'll just try a few more, I whisper, and swipe away.

Almost every time I swipe to the right, there's a match.

That's unbelievable, I mumble. Is this some sort of El Dorado?

My cellphone keeps dinging, I'm getting all stressed. Seeing my face colliding with men's faces. Getting messages from them. There are probably a lot more men than women on here, I imagine.

I pull my hands through my greasy hair. I can't manage to keep up and reply to them all. That's probably what you're supposed to do, I muse.

I reply to the guy with the long black hair, and we agree to meet at Bartof Café the next day.

I already see him from the street reflected in a big mirror inside the café. I stop and watch him. He swings his hair that reaches down to the middle of his upper arms and gathers it in a man bun at the back of his head. Then I set in motion again and turn the corner and enter.

He gets up as I approach him. We smile shyly, hug each other.

Great meeting you, he says.

With an accent from west Jutland.

Thank you, the same to you, I say.

We sit down and are silent for a while. I'm contemplating what we could talk about.

Are you a Sikh? I say.

A Sikh? he says, and opens his eyes wide.

Yes, except that you're not wearing a turban now, I say.

He grabs his head with both hands.

You look like the Sikhs in Arusha in Tanzania where I lived, I say.

I'm not a Sikh, he says.

In any case, I was quite fascinated by their masculinity, I add.

Was it special? he says.

Yes, it was. They had a particular, straightforward way of looking me in the eye, and a proud and rolling gait.

I'm a Kurd, he says. From Esbjerg. Or, strictly speaking, my father was a Kurd.

Ah, okay, that makes sense. There's the same kind of pride in that culture, I say.

It doesn't take long before my fingers are in the Kurd's hair, and it doesn't take long either before we are lying in my bed. In spite of our seventeen year age difference.

I discover that young men by and large are surprisingly interested in older women. Many of my subsequent Tinder dates are very young men, and consequently when I tell Anne about a new date, she always asks with some apprehension:

How old is he?

That there could be something between younger men and older women has gone right over my head. I've of course seen *The Graduate* and Bo Widerberg's *All Things Fair*, but I always imagined the phenomenon was much less common than what I'm experiencing now. And I believed it was a mistake when young men checked me out.

Ida also told me that one evening when she crossed the square by Nørreport Station, a group of young guys had their eyes on her. She heard them say MILF, after which her cellphone and Google came to her rescue: *Mom I'd like to fuck*. Later on we also learn the word *cougar*.

Young men know a thing or two.

The Kurd, for example, gives me my first squirting when we lie upstairs in my bed that evening.

I don't understand what he's doing. He has two fingers inside me, is bent over me, and moves his fingers vigorously, his entire arm, he shakes me while I look at him in wonder.

Suddenly fluid squirts out of me, it keeps coming, most of his arm is wet as if he had inseminated a cow, his beard and face are wet, the bed is a mess. We have to spread towels over the bed to be able to lie on it afterwards.

On following dates, the men only have to touch me and it starts squirting from me, it flows onto the floor—"Look how you're squirting, honey!" It never ceases to fascinate, the Kurd has opened something, and I'm still full of surprise.

Anne says she has read in the daily *Information* that it's pee, but I don't believe it, it doesn't smell like it, and it's completely transparent.

Sønder Vilstrup, Jutland
1977 and 1982

I don't learn how to read until I'm in Grade 4. The teachers at Eltang Central School are discussing whether I might be slow, and they want me to take special education classes together with Mogens. But my parents don't want me in the special education classes. They are of the opinion that if they continue reading to me, the problem will resolve itself.

It never occurs to me that there is a problem. I'm hanging upside down in a tree.

They don't tell me until several years later.

I learn how to read because I want to read Hans Kirk's novel *The Fishermen*. It's being shown on TV as a series when I'm ten years old, and it's one of the few programs we are allowed to watch. We're ready and waiting, once a week. When the series is over, I find the book in my father's bookcase and gobble it up.

From now on I go to his study every time I've finished reading a novel, and then we crawl slowly along the bookcases to find the next one suitable for me to read. He asks me what it should be about, and it doesn't take long before I feel like saying: Sex and love. But I don't say it. I try to disguise it in vague terms and say: Something about people, something about their relationships.

The first books he gives me after *The Fishermen* are works by Tarjei Vesaas. I start making a list of the titles I have read.

Tarjei Vesaas: *The Winds, Spring Night, The Birds*
Jakob Paludan: *Birds Around the Light*
Knut Hamsun: *Pan, Victoria, Hunger, The Growth of the Soil*
Jakob Knudsen: *Temperament, Unrest-Clarity*
Selma Lagerlöf: *The Saga of Gösta Berling, The Löwensköld Ring*
Sigrid Undset: *Kristin Lavransdatter, Olav Audunssøn, Jenny*
Martin A. Hansen: *The Liar*
Ingmar Bergman's screenplay of *Persona*
Henrik Pontoppidan: *Lucky Per*
Jens Peter Jacobsen: *Niels Lyhne, Marie Grubbe*[8]

But one day I come across a wonderful book in a box in a second-hand bookshop. It's called *Charlotte* and it's written by Ib Henrik Cavling. The cover has a picture of a beautiful, red-headed woman. It reminds me of the drawings on the front covers of Anne's *Golden Love Tales*. So already I know I'll have to pop it into my school bag and keep it a secret. I find some brown wrapping paper and make a new dust jacket so I can read it regardless of where I am. It's not only my father who should be kept in the dark about my reading a book with a cover like that. It's the same as with masturbation. It's impossible to not do it even if it's shameful, not only in the eyes of my father and the whole world but also to me.

In high school I read Tage Skou-Hansen's novel *The Naked Trees*, and I'm completely turned on by Gerda's passion. Saturday morning I sit at the long dining table with my mother and father and defend Gerda's right to be unfaithful because her love and passion for Holger is so strong. When strong feelings like that are at work, I say, I believe they transcend her moral obligation to her husband.

My mother listens attentively and keeps on asking me questions. My father does the same. He's relaxed, his face calm. He says he agrees with me.

Several years later Anne tells me our mother had a relationship with Tage Skou-Hansen while being married to our father. That she even became pregnant with him but had an abortion.

While Anne is telling me this, I remember my father's relaxed face and that he thought I was right.

Wow, I say to Anne, well done!

Yes, she says.

Frederiksberg Neighbourhood in Copenhagen
October 2016

Cognitive Johnny puts his backpack on a dining chair and sits down on the chair beside it. He unzips the backpack.

Do you want a ginger lozenge? he says, and passes me the box.

Yes, thank you, I say, and take one.

The last time he was here, he gave me a worksheet titled ADJUSTING THE RULES FOR LIVING. *Personal rules that distinguish between "right" and "wrong" are formed through personal experience. These are often outdated rules that maintain the status quo and work against one's own best interests.*

Under the rubric MY OLD RULE IS, I've written:

I'm dependent on having a boyfriend.

Next it says: THE RULE HAS HAD THE FOLLOWING CONSEQUENCES IN MY LIFE. *Describe briefly what impact this rule has had on you and your life.*

I've written: I become far too dependent on my boyfriend while we're together. I become anxious when he leaves me.

Next rubric: I KNOW THE RULE IS AT RISK WHEN:

Here I've written: I believe I'm not connected to the world when I don't have a boyfriend. I feel anxious. I fight to get my boyfriend back or to find a new one. I feel the world is an insecure place. I feel lonely.

Two things are important if I'm going to get better: I must be able to write and also try to get rid of this unreasonable notion. And I'm determined to get well. So I'll buckle down, although it seems to me these reflections are rather elementary.

The next rubric says: IT IS UNDERSTANDABLE THAT THIS RULE EXISTS BECAUSE (summarize the experiences that led to the creation of the rule and that have maintained it).

I've written: Early loss. Anxiety throughout my childhood. Loneliness. No friends during childhood.

That's good, Cognitive Johnny says, after he has read the whole thing. He begins to gather up his papers and markers and puts them in his bag.

Shouldn't I have a ginger lozenge? I say.

Café Viggo
Værnedamsvej
Frederiksberg Neighbourhood in Copenhagen
October 2016

Ida knows a place on Værnedamsvej called Viggo. It's a kind of provincial restaurant with a dance floor. There are no interesting men here, we only come to dance.

We sit in the bar area that's packed with people, we're being observed.

Ida always speaks in a loud, slow, and clear tone:

How do you take care of your intimate hygiene? she says.

I flinch and look around me. Everyone has heard it.

Or, rather, your shaving method, she says.

It's completely natural for Ida to use a word like *rather*. The men around us take it all in their stride.

I lean closer to Ida.

I shave every day, I whisper. I remove everything and just leave a small triangle. Brazilian, I think it's called.

I think I need some help with it, she says.

Yes?

Just the first time, she says. It's quite a task to undertake.

I can't tolerate waxing, I say. I tried getting my eyebrows waxed. It pulled off the skin.

Ouch, Ida says.

So I'm not brave enough to do the pussy, I say.

Ida shakes her head.

No, don't do that! she says.

Yeah, I say.

We sip some beer.

Hey, Ida says.

What? I say.

When we're ready to have boyfriends again, she says, we'll have to look for somebody who wouldn't think of us as being too wild or violent or weird.

I grab her arm that's resting on the bar.

Exactly, I say. It's insane how much energy you and I have spent on trying to change ourselves.

In fact, it's a form of brainwashing that we've been exposed to, she says.

And the creepy thing is, I say, you don't notice it while it's going on. It sneaks up on you. You lose touch with yourself and what you feel like doing and what you don't feel like doing. If I occasionally sensed that something wasn't good for me, I would just tell myself that my feelings aren't to be trusted.

Ida nods.

That's what I thought was happening with you, she says.

And then it's completely impossible to orient yourself, I say.

It is, she says.

I'm so fucking sick of the thought that I've let myself go that far, I say.

There's good energy in that feeling, she says, and reaches out for her beer.

At the same time I can still sink into a bottomless longing for Jan, I say.

Ida looks at me. Then she lets out a deep sigh.

Frederiksberg Neighbourhood in Copenhagen
November 2016

Cognitive Johnny has said I should praise myself all the time.

So that's what I do:

Well done, Karen! I say in a loud voice, sounding impressed after I've put a cup in the dishwasher. Way to go!

Eventually, only when I've put seven cups, five glasses, and six plates away. Well done, Karen! I say. Or when I've translated a novel or written three pages. Or when a man who I like a lot doesn't want to see me any longer, and I take it relatively calmly. Excellent, Karen! I say. You handled that well!

Finally I forget to say: Well done, Karen, way to go!

*

I'm twelve years old when I decide what I want to be when I grow up, I want to be a writer. I'm not telling anyone. It's not something you can talk about to others. And especially not to my father. He still talks excitedly about the great writers he met while teaching at Askov Folk High School. I sense that they all flocked to the place: Tage Skou-Hansen, Thorkild Bjørnvig, Frank Jæger. His tone changes when he talks about them, and I understand that they are not necessarily human beings. It has to do with a special mode of being in the world. Almost godlike, I suspect. The same goes for what they generate. Their books in his bookcases. The ruler-straight underlining, the exclamation marks, and his added comments.

I, myself, am a human being. This I know for sure. And that's why I understand very well that I'm aspiring to something beyond my own realm if I wish to be a writer.

But I can't stop writing. I write and I write. Fragments and dialogues. And there's no time of day when I'm more happy than when I sit in my room at my desk that is pushed right up against the dormer window and write. I have feelings of absolute presence and absolute absence at the same time. Of giving my all. The way I think ballet dancers do when I watch them on TV.

I don't tell anyone what I'm doing. It's almost like masturbating or dressing up in my mother's high heels.

But when I'm eighteen I show my father a long text I've written. Ten pages. It's the longest continuous text I've written so far.

He makes himself comfortable in the easy chair in the corner by one of the bookcases. With his reading glasses and my sheets of paper.

I walk back and forth in the dining room. Look at the clock. Slip outside for a minute. Return to pacing back and forth in the dining room.

At last he enters. He stands in the centre of the room with his reading glasses in one hand and my sheets of paper in the other. I'm standing ramrod straight, watching him.

Then he says:

That's probably a good way to overcome unrequited love.

Everything inside me sinks. I look at him. Then I look down.

Yes, I say.

He puts the sheets of paper on the dining table and returns to his easy chair in the other room and to the novel he was reading.

I don't write anymore.

Over the years I feel increasingly inflamed. Images and sense perceptions are absorbed by the blotting paper that I've become. But they remain hidden inside me like a raging infection. And when I watch ballet dancers on TV—their sweat, their fatigue, their worn bodies—I feel this profound hunger for being able to give my all like I once did.

But every time the infection is about to rupture my skin, I bandage the inflamed red spots with gauze and hide them from sight. Right up to the time, ten years later, when I'm about to write my thesis at university and instead begin writing literary texts again.

I don't tell anyone that I have sent the texts to the Danish Academy of Creative Writing. They accept me.

Then I phone my father.

He's silent, and then he speaks, slowly and in a tone I've never heard him use with me before.

Two and a half years later, my first novel comes out. I pull it out of the bookcase one day when I'm back home visiting. Inside are exclamation marks and comments in the margins and passages underlined with a ruler.

For the next five years, a special calmness prevails between my father and me.

Then he dies.

PART
FIVE

Stolpegård Psychotherapy Centre
Vangede
Greater Copenhagen Area
November 2016

I've wished for this for a long time, and it's finally coming true: Stolpegård's unit for the treatment of personality disorders has a spot for me.

The waiting area with the terracotta-tiled floor is full of women and a few men. A psychologist comes out, and by reading names out loud from a sheet of paper, she picks out those of us who have to follow her. People stand up, and we walk behind her through long hallways until we reach a room equipped with yet another oval conference table.

The psychologist projects words onto the screen in front of us. We're having a lesson in psychoeducation. We need a better understanding of our various personality disorders.

I'm once again able to process a long train of thoughts, and I soak up the words on the screen and those that come out of her mouth. I write and write. A young woman at the end of the table is telling us about having a fight with somebody at a bus stop the previous day. I look at her but soon bend over my notes again. I have my own project to do here.

I learn that a definitive trait of my diagnosis consists of different forms of lapses in my ability to mentalize.

I have plenty of empathy and ability to put myself in other people's shoes and understand situations from their point of view. Almost too much. Overmentalization, the psychologist calls it. It's a weakness in my mentalizing ability. You need to be able to turn off and not constantly relate to and make sense of everything and everyone. It's hard on a person, and it leads to situations where you're at the mercy of your emotions and lose the capacity for rational understanding of circumstances and relationships.

It was especially with Jan that my emotional apparatus geared up. When, for instance, I didn't hear from him for an entire day, the internal factory got rolling, the whole thermodynamic system set in motion. The furnaces were fed with coal, the fire would blaze, the heat would increase, the steam would rise, the cogwheels would turn and engage with each other. Not only was I a big machine that generated a roar of emotions, but I also did not have any filters. Everything engulfed and saturated me.

Right up to the point where the red-hot machine began to melt down and everything collapsed, and intense emotions came rushing over me like an army of termites chewing the flesh off my bones.

When I return home from psychoeducation, I continue with some reading. Walk back and forth in the living room and think. I've come a long way now, but I want to go further.

I want to reach the place where I dare to engage in a love relationship while at the same time being able to sit calmly with my hands in my lap, watching and listening without turning into a rumbling, emotional machine. To the place where I feel intact.

Underhuset
Vesterbro Neighbourhood in Copenhagen
December 2016

Ida and I meet on Halmtorvet in front of Underhuset, where we go dancing from time to time. There's a long lineup. Ida walks up to the doorman and asks how long it will take before we can get in. As it always happens around Ida, a lot of chatting and laughing can be heard, and I'm standing here at the back of the lineup, overwhelmed with love for her.

She returns.

One and a half hours, she says.

Obviously we don't feel like waiting that long, so we head over to Mandela next door. They have live jazz.

We buy beer and squeeze ourselves into a spot in the crowded place.

Have you seen Adam lately? I ask.

Adam is Ida's lover. She has only one at a time.

No, I'm trying to take a break from him, she says. I began waiting for his text messages.

Ah, I say.

And that won't work, she says.

I shake my head.

I was thinking of you, I say, when I biked past his apartment on my way over here. I was thinking that perhaps you were also biking that way.

She nods.

I was, she says.

The light was on, I say.

I noticed that, she says. I don't think I would have been able to resist the temptation if I had had my intimate shaving under control.

I'm about to say something, but she raises her eyebrows and turns toward me.

By the way, she says, sugaring, you should give it a try!

What is it? I ask.

Ida is way ahead of me.

It's more gentle than waxing, she says. I don't think it'll pull the skin off your pussy.

Really? I say cheerfully. I'll try it for sure.

But it still feels like your pussy is being ripped off, she adds.

I cross my legs.

The lineup by Underhuset is still long, so we walk around the corner of the building, where there's an outdoor smoking area surrounded by a tall fence. But there are a couple of stones you can step onto. We grab hold of the fence from opposite sides, and our heads become visible to the people inside.

They turn toward us.

What the hell! they say.

Straddling the fence, I look down at a bunch of laughing faces and arms that reach out to me. Ida is already being lowered on the other side. I aim for the arms that look most capable and end up standing in the middle of the crowd.

Thank you, I say, and bend down to check if my tights have ripped.

There's a tear all the way down the back of my thigh.

Ida walks over to me and digs out a pack of smokes from her purse. She hands me one. I buy us each a beer at the small outdoor bar.

Cheers, I say, raising the plastic cup in her direction.

We lean against the fence while smoking. The men who lifted us down are looking at us. I slip my arm through hers.

Come, I say, let's dance.

The small space is packed with people, everyone is dancing, hardly anyone is at the bar. We squeeze ourselves into a spot in the middle of the chaos where we can dance. It's hot. I notice the back of a man whose shirt is soaking wet, sweat forming a T pattern across his shoulder blades and down his spine. His hair looks black and shiny from the dampness, and the dark grey tattoo of a scorpion that winds around his upper arm glistens from the sweat. His upper body rocks back and forth, and when he turns a little I can see his broad smile and a face that radiates happiness.

I lean toward Ida.

Too bad the guy over there is with her, I say.

Ida turns to look at him.

His energy is wild, I say.

Sønder Vilstrup, Jutland
The 1970s

My dollhouse is absolutely wonderful. It has two floors and furniture I can move around. And then there are three Bendi dolls and a small, stiff baby. The baby is useless, but the Bendi dolls...! If you bend it at its waist, you can put its head into your private parts while its toes touch the small hard knob I've discovered I have just above it.

Why do you wash the doll? my mother asks one day when I'm in the bathroom, scrubbing it under the tap. It takes on a strong odour if I don't.

As time goes by, I find out I can write stories that I then read while stuffing one of the dolls in my pussy. It has an unheard-of effect.

But one day we make a strange discovery. We've biked down to Allégården—Anne, her girlfriend Birgitte, a couple of other kids, and me. The farmhouse is empty, the barns too. But from a beam in the coach house hangs a horse.

We jump off the bikes, rest our arms on the handlebars, and stare at it. We had heard it had died, but we don't know why it's hanging there.

The horse had been in the field with a cow. I had seen them grazing on my way home from school. But one day I heard that the horse had gone mad, all of Sønder Vilstrup was talking about it. The horse had killed the cow. No one knows why, but it bit the cow's throat, pure and simple.

Afterwards one of the men put a bullet to its head. We don't know where the cow ended up, but in any case, the horse is hanging here.

We park the bikes and sneak past it into the cowshed. Old hay lies scattered in the stalls. The cowshed is bigger than our barns and not quite as rundown. I walk down the manure gutter. Suddenly I notice a bulging plastic bag stuffed with magazines. I squat down and pull one of them out. I open it and see a picture of something, I've no idea what it is. I see a woman's face with something incomprehensible in her wide-open mouth. I've seen my father's penis a few times, and Niels's. When swimming in a mountain lake, for instance. And even though my father's penis is considerably bigger than Niels's, he's an adult after all, this thing is something very different. It's huge and appears hard, almost distended. On the sides are thick veins. And the woman has it in her mouth! That's the most perplexing thing of all. My stomach feels queasy, and nausea rises to my mouth. I bend over and throw up.

A few years later I begin masturbating to Erica Jong's *Fanny*. The book has moved from my father's bookcase to my room, where it's hidden away in a plastic bag under my socks in the bottom drawer of my dresser. I know exactly which passages are the best, and when I'm ready, the book opens by itself to those pages.

But I would also like to have some pictures to look at, and I've noticed that Bent Shopkeeper has some porno magazines sitting on the lower shelf of his little magazine rack. Or rather, there's just one porno magazine. *The Weekly Report*, it's called. But entering the store, picking up the magazine, and placing it on Bent Shopkeeper's counter is out of the question. So for a long time I mull over how I can get the magazine out of the store.

I consider various possibilities and reach the conclusion that the only solution is to steal it.

I've never stolen anything from a store before, and I'm scared witless.

The day I've decided to do it, my heart is pounding under my parka as I bike home from school. The entire six kilometres with sweaty palms inside my mittens. But I'm hell-bent on doing it, I park the bike outside, walk into the store, nod to Bent Shopkeeper, who's sitting at his desk in the backroom, say I'm going to look around a bit, after which I take a stroll around the very small store and end by the magazine rack, and quick as a flash I bend down, grab the magazine, stuff it in my school bag, and stand up straight. I look around. No one has seen it. I slip out the door.

My pulse is pounding in my throat, and I lean all the way forward on the bike to gain maximum speed.

I keep the magazine hidden in my old school bag and put it in the bottom of my closet toward the very back. Here it'll be safe. Until the day my mother and I can't find my exercise book, and she begins searching for it all over my room. She works quickly, goes through the room systematically. Pulls out drawers, sifts through them, opens the closet, and ends up sitting on her knees by the bottom shelf. I watch her pulling the school bag out, I'm desperate, searching my brain for something plausible to say to prevent her from unlocking the bag. But I don't manage to find something to say. I've very little time to think.

I shout:

No, not that one, Mom!

She turns around, alarmed, and looks at me.

I stare at her with a wild look in my eyes. Can't find anything else to say. But she lets go of the bag, slowly, and puts it back in the closet.

Frederiksberg Neighbourhood in Copenhagen
January 2017

It's windy. I can tell from the large birch tree below my window. And I can hear it. The wind is rattling the windowpanes and muntin bars, it's hissing through the cracks. I like the sound. As if big trees were spinning like whisks above my head. I touch the cool glass with my forehead and realize I'm not anxious.

I straighten up. Take one step back.

I'm alone, there are no distractions, and there is no anxiety.

In my head are calm, clear thoughts.

I'm in the process of translating the Norwegian writer Vigdis Hjorth's *Arv og miljø* into Danish.[9] It's a novel, but the Norwegian critics have been busy adding two and two together and are of the opinion that it's autofiction or reality literature, as they call it in Norway. They compare the novel with her earlier texts, in which she describes her time undergoing psychoanalysis. It's clear to them that the text is about her own life. But in this novel there's something new: Her father's abusive behaviour. In Norway there are heated discussions about ethics. The father is dead. What if the abuse isn't true? If it has never happened? What if it's true and it actually *did* happen?

I still don't feel any anxiety. But it can come on at any time.

I walk around the apartment. Shake my hands, my arms. Stop and check again.

It's not coming on.

My anxiety skin is gone. Anxiety skin is thick, heavy. Difficult to move under. And at the same time light and fluttery. It leads you around, has its own pathways. Usually through cold, foggy landscapes. Rushing headlong after a boyfriend. Heels not touching the ground. Insteps dragged across floors and streets. Weighs nothing. Can be lugged around. There are hunger holes in the skin instead of eyes. Everything passes through the holes. The exchange is fierce, going at a furious pace. The much too heavy and the much too airy sensations form a unity.

Anxiety has been my basic emotional state for seven months. There's nothing I fear more than anxiety. Anxiety is the constant sound of gnashing rat teeth. The beast in my belly.

Next morning I wake up, open my eyes, lie still, and look around the room. Is it here?

It isn't.

Sønder Vilstrup and Kolding, Jutland
The 1970s and 1980s

I have a feeling I'm not going to survive, and I know that if I want to survive, it's up to me to make sure it happens.

I'm eleven years old and take gymnastics. My trainer is not only good at doing three flips in a row diagonally across the floor, he's also kind, and I'm especially lucky for being sway-backed. So I'm frequently pulled aside and asked to do special exercises with him. He kneels in front of me, places one hand on my lower back and the other on my stomach, then pushes in on my abdomen and the sway lessens.

Can you feel it in your body? he says.

I nod in silence.

That's the sensation you should aim for, he continues.

I give him a serious look when he gets up on his feet.

Don't be sad, he says.

I shake my head vigorously. Because I'm not sad. I'm full of happiness. But I can't say that, so I just keep on shaking my head.

I'm sure it will correct itself, he says, if you practise that sensation.

I never manage to pull myself together to ask if I could live at his place, and then two years later, when the bullying becomes so bad that I also experience it at gymnastics, I quit going altogether.

I'm a stone you throw in water; I set the surface in motion, and the girls slip away from me like ripples spreading across the pond.

But a new possibility arises. I change schools in the eighth grade and attend Kolding School, where my homeroom teacher tells us his newborn son's name is going to be Hurricane.

I think it's wonderful that his son is going to be named Hurricane, and I practise pronouncing it just as expertly as he does.

During his lessons no one is slumped over their desk half asleep. We sit up straight and are wide awake, waiting for the next hilarious thing he'll say. And when he passes me on his way to the teacher's desk and puts his hand on my shoulder, I feel something akin to spasms in my chest.

For several months I contemplate whether it would be proper to approach him and tell him how I feel. In the end I decide that it would. I've no clear idea of what he could possibly do about it, but every time he talks about his son whose name will be Hurricane, and I see his eyes light up whenever he talks about him, I become more and more convinced that there *must* be something he can do.

But I don't dare talk to him without my mother giving me permission first.

So, one day I pluck up my courage and ask her:
Mom?
She is sitting on the sofa, reading *Kolding Folkeblad*.
Yes?
I've been thinking that I would like to talk to my homeroom teacher about how I'm feeling, about how we're managing here at home.

235

She lowers the paper. Then she says:

Don't you dare!

I don't.

When I'm in my first year of high school, I have a girlfriend for the first time.

I'm sixteen and stand naked in the locker room after gym class, and suddenly she says:

You have a gorgeous body.

I tense up. No one has said anything like that to me before.

She gives me a serious look.

From then on we become inseparable, talking during every recess, and even sleeping over at each other's house.

But one day my mother says that my girlfriend is honey-tongued and there's something catlike about her. Only the two of us are in the room, my mother is sitting at the head of the dining table, and I'm sitting close to her on the long side. She's in a good mood, and we're having a nice time together.

I love my girlfriend but get angry with her for being the way my mother says. I haven't thought of it myself, but now that my mother has mentioned it, I believe it too, and I sit down by my typewriter and write her a long letter. I write that I think she is honey-tongued and catlike.

But a year later I'm no longer a nice child.

Those large eyes of mine—that would look and look at my mother and father in order to figure out who I should be—have now become narrow, desperate slits that have ceased to look.

I'm standing inside my shell and spin around in the cold fog that permeates the space in here. There are many of us, we're being sucked backwards out of the world and into here, and I panic at the claws and the rasping tongue that hollows us out from the inside.

I smash glasses and plates, I'm tears, I'm despair, I'm anger pouring out of my mouth like vomit.

Anne has moved to Copenhagen.

There's no longer anyone here to make the beast calm down.

My mother and father hold down the mad child.

My father holds my arms and my mother pushes my head back. I can't wriggle out of their grasp, and she takes hold of my jaws, she adds pressure to force my mouth open. My father tightens his grip. My mother pours akvavit into my open mouth, and I swallow and I swallow.

Karen has to be sedated.

At regular intervals I scream at my mother that I don't want to live at home anymore.

But I'm afraid of the beast in my belly. I'm afraid of how it might show up if I live alone in a rented room in Kolding; hence my threats are but empty words.

Until the day when she says:

It's just something you're saying. You'll never go through with it.

I don't answer. I walk out of the living room and upstairs to my father in his study. He calls his cousin in Kolding, and I move into a room in their house.

I arrange the room nicely, all eight square metres of it, and invite my new friends for dinner, Casper and Michael and Rose and Christian. We sit squeezed together around my desk and drink beer and eat, we listen to The Doors and discuss politics, but when I need something from the kitchen, I stand by the door and listen for my father's cousin and her husband. I don't dare go out there if they are around.

Rose gives me a white teapot as a housewarming gift, and I cut off my long hair, buy a knee-length army coat from the army surplus store, and take up smoking.

Rose and I lie on the bed, which is far too small for two people. We share the last smoke in the pack before going to sleep.

I play hooky from school, I receive warnings, my high grades plummet.

The teachers are concerned.

Where has Karen, the good student, gone? they say.

I find myself bending over the abyss inside me, I don't know where this is going, if it's going to the dogs.

One evening after a high school party I knock about on the roads around the school, which is located on the outskirts of town.

I've decided I don't want to live anymore. I've decided to take my own life. I stand on the shoulder of a wide road where the cars drive fast. When a bus drives by, I'll throw myself in front of it.

I wait for a long time, it's cold, I'm shaking.

But when the bus comes, I don't throw myself in front of it, I jump back into the ditch.

There I lie, staring up at the sky.

Then I get up.

I just thought of a last possibility, six years after I first had the idea.

I walk over to Kolding Højskole, which is next to my high school. I continue on to one of the flats in the teachers' quarters. I stand outside the door. My parents' friends live in there. The woman is a teacher at Kolding Højskole, but the husband is a psychologist.

Anne and Niels and I have always liked them.

The husband had once asked my parents if they had remembered to give the new brood of stressed chickens plenty of straw so they would settle down in the barn.

He can help me.

I'm standing in front of the door.

It's nighttime.

It's not very considerate to call on people in the middle of the night.

The following day I phone my father.

I want to move back home again, I say.

My voice is high-pitched, emerging from the upper, panicky part of my throat.

Yes? he says.

Preferably right away, I say.

You're welcome to come back, he says.

He says he'll pick me up tomorrow.

No, I almost scream, please pick me up right now!

Three years later I'm sitting on top of a table in a house where Anne is working as a housecleaner. I've moved to Copenhagen and have gone over to help her with the work.

I use the word *insecure*.

I say I've felt insecure all my life.

But Anne suddenly calls it something different.

She calls it anxiety.

Of course I know the word. As a child I heard my father talk about it in connection with literature. We use it in Comparative Literature at the university where I'm studying now and where we have read Rilke's *The Notebooks of Malte Laurids Brigge*, which made me nauseous. I've read about it in all those books on psychology and psychoanalysis I'm always plowing through.

But it never occurred to me that the word could have any relevance to me.

You have suffered from anxiety, Anne says.

The word makes me go to pieces like I've never gone to pieces before.

I can't get a grip on myself.

Animal-like, screaming, sobbing sounds emerge from my throat.

Anne takes me back to her place. Wraps me in blankets, sits beside me.

Then she calls a psychoanalyst.

20a Restaurant and Kind of Blue Bar
Ravnsborggade
Nørrebro Neighbourhood in Copenhagen
February 2017

I have trouble keeping up with my laundry. I have four pillow covers, four duvet covers, and two sheets that are all used in a rotation system. I'm thinking of biking to Ikea to top up my supply.

I have a small team of carefully selected Tinder lovers, and then the incidental ones along the way. It's working out fine. Apart from the problem with the bed linen.

But one day a man writes to me, saying he has second thoughts about meeting me because he has googled my name and found out I'm sick.

On my next date I decide I better tell the new guy before he finds out for himself.

He's a Swedish actor and dancer and not that much younger than me, it's all acceptable. We're meeting at Restaurant 20a in Ravnsborggade. I've made a reservation for two at the tall table by the window. The small room is comfortably warm, there's a candle on the table, I have a glass of wine, I'm happy, I feel free.

The Swede walks through the door. I turn around in my chair and reach out to him.

Hi, I say.

He looks at me, then he opens his mouth with a broad smile, showing his big teeth. Mine does the same, and the entire evening the two of us sit side by side with two sets of wide, smiling mouths and two sets of big teeth.

I feel I'm looking into my own face, I say, when I look into yours.

After we've shared a bottle of wine, he puts his hands on my hips and pulls me onto his lap.

I jump down. People are enjoying their tapas and red wine.

Come, I say, let's go over there.

I nod toward Kind of Blue on the other side of the street.

He grabs his coat, and we cross the street holding hands.

We manage to squeeze ourselves into a spot at the bar. The place is packed. They are playing "Freddie Freeloader."

He repeats the manoeuvre right away, and this time I stay on his lap. He looks at me, peering intensely into my eyes.

I really want you, I say.

Same here, he says.

I stroke his cheek with my index finger.

It's too far to go to my place, he says.

Yes, I say.

Can we go to your place?

No, I say.

I could easily fall in love with this guy, so I have to be careful.

He shakes his head slowly.

But I would like to see you again, I say.

I would also like to see you again, he says.

He texts me while I'm on my bike going home to Frederiksberg. He writes that it feels like he's already fallen in love with me and wants to know when we can meet again.

242

When I'm home, I write that we can see each other in two days. But that I'll have to tell him I have BPD. That I don't like the idea of him finding out for himself in case he should start googling me. I write that I've been sick but no longer am. I tell him about my friend who is bipolar and who says he believes people like us are actually easier to get on with than so many others because we've been forced in a terrifying way to look ourselves deep in the eye and face our darkest fears and difficulties. And have learned to manage them.

He answers me:

I have to be completely honest, Karen, and say that I'm not brave enough to take you on.

*

"There are people who wear a face for years, and of course it wears away, gets dirty, cracks in the creases. Other people change their faces uncannily quickly, one after the other, and wear them out."[10] My father carries all his faces with him. He doesn't wear the old one out before adapting a new one. He makes quick changes, every day. All his faces are in use, and he has many at his disposal.

And yet, when he gets older I discover that some of them must have been worn out and discarded. I don't see them anymore. The insane, the furious, the mocking, the jeering, those that are fighting themselves and have slack lips and twitching around their eyes. They are the oldest, the ones he carried with him from far back, from the era of the puritan patriarch.

The faces that are left are those that listen and watch with all twenty-four muscles engaged at the same time. Those that face the pain of a lifetime without falling apart.

Fifteen months after my father dies, my mother becomes ill. She is sixty-six and dies half a year later.

The first thing I feel when I hear the diagnosis is shame and regret. For having punished her so harshly.

When I was young, there were periods when I didn't want to see her.

And still she came with my father to hear my first reading in Kolding. I had just published my first novel, and my father, always the Danish teacher, had sent me a long letter with an enthusiastic text analysis and had asked with some apprehension if the father in the novel was him.

No, I answered, it's fiction.

My mother didn't ask if the mother in the novel was her.

I send her a text message. I don't write anything about that. I write about my best memory of her. Tell her how happy I was when we went down to Bent Shopkeeper at the Co-op and bought mackerel in tomato sauce and a tube of mayonnaise and white bread sprinkled with poppy seeds and we ate the whole thing while watching TV.

Now she's the one who suffers from anxiety. She has lung cancer that has spread to the cerebellum. Anne, Niels, and I take turns going to Odense University Hospital. Every third day one of us leaves the house at eight o'clock in the morning and returns home at eleven at night.

A tube, thick as a finger, disappears between her ribs. Next to the bed hangs a transparent bag with yellowish brown fluid from her lungs. She throws up, constantly. I rinse her upper bridge with its false teeth and try to eat up her anxiety.

After two months, part of the time in intensive care, where my mother is connected to tubes and breathes through her big open mouth, Anne manages to put pressure on the medical staff to have her transferred to Rigshospitalet, the state hospital in Copenhagen, where she'll receive stereotactic radiation treatment on her cerebellum. So that she won't throw up all the time, and she'll be able to stand more securely on her feet. But it doesn't prevent her from dying soon.

We talk about who should go with her. Anne has to work at the university, Niels cannot cope with it, it'll be me.

It's early in the morning and still dark when I go to see her at the hospital. Rain hangs obliquely in the air outside. She's sitting up in her bed. She's composed now. I'm composed. Together we'll deal with this. A porter collects her, wheels the bed into the elevator that takes us deep down into the basement under the hospital. I walk beside the bed. We walk along the subterranean corridors with their wide yellow stripes on the floor and parked trolley carts with bedpans. There are pipes under the ceilings. I don't understand how the porter orients himself here. We reach an area that opens into a larger space. There are chairs and tables, ficus trees. Here people can sit and wait.

We continue into a room with machines I haven't seen before. A man wearing jeans and a T-shirt walks in, he's a doctor. In the underworld you don't wear a white coat.

My mother is placed in a chair, and the doctor draws four X's, two on her forehead, two on the back of her head. When he sticks a hypodermic needle into the X's in her forehead, they swell up. I'm squatting in front of her. My arms are on her thighs, I fix my eyes on her. The doctor lowers a wide metal frame over her head.

It weighs two kilos, he says.

It has four holes. He inserts a screw into one of them and with a Phillips screwdriver he pulls out of his back pocket, he tightens it into the red X in the skin of her forehead and into her skull.

The only thing for us to do now is to continue to fix our eyes on each other.

Then the next screw. She's whimpering. The anaesthetic isn't working as it should in all the spots.

The doctor holds the last two screws between his lips. Removes them one at a time and screws them in. The iron crown is now fastened to her head.

She is wheeled to the scanning area, after which a computer will calculate precisely where the radiation has to go.

I'm standing in the empty waiting room with the ficus trees. Walking in cicles. There's a washroom. I go in there. Gather my hair in my hand and throw up. Sit down and bend over, my forehead touching the cold floor. When the dizziness passes, I go out to meet her.

She's beaming under her iron crown. It's all done with. The porter wheels her back under the ceiling pipes, and we end up in her room again.

Anne rushes in, she has finished her teaching, I meet her in the hallway. Hold on to her tightly.

The anaesthetic wasn't working as it should, I say.

Anne holds my head between her hands.

We go in. Sit down on either side of the bed. Our mother is sitting straight up under her crown.

Anne turns pale.

You look like Jesus, she says, with the crown of thorns.

Frederiksberg Neighbourhood in Copenhagen
March 2017

When I was a child, I wrote without anxiety. I wrote my first novel without anxiety. The subsequent novels and short stories, however, were squeezed out through anxiety pores in my skin that were much too small. But now there's neither skin nor anxiety between the non-materialized writing inside me and the words that trickle out onto the screen in front of me. We're one, a single flow, and I'm limitless.

Not Malte Laurids Brigge's limitlessness, not the limitlessness that creates anxiety. I have my own skin now, I'm inside it. And my blood vessels are free of friction. They stretch from someplace behind my eyes and all the way out through my arms to my fingertips, from where the words fall in droplets.

I start cancelling my dates. I don't feel like going. I'm not feeling well, have caught the flu, I write.

I hang on to two of them. A diplomat defected from Hungary with whom I discuss politics. And a psychologist employed in the psychiatric field with whom I discuss psychology and psychiatry. I like talking with them but would actually prefer not having to make love to them.

One day I say to Anne that I could probably fall in love with the diplomat, the next day I say I could probably fall in love with the psychologist.

As you know, I'm feeling well now, I add, I do my work, translate and write. And my life is fine without a boyfriend.

We walk around The Lakes.

Mission accomplished? Anne says.

The pact has been realized, I say.

But I suppose you don't have to fall in love right away? Anne says, and gives me an inquisitive look.

No, I say, but I see it as work that has to be done, and I might as well get it over with.

Hmm, she says.

Maybe it's not possible to fall in love anymore, I say, at my age.

What do I know, she says, I've been married for ages.

The following day Niels is sitting on my couch. I'm standing in the middle of the room.

I think I could fall in love with the psychologist, I say.

He screws up his eyes.

I don't believe it, Karen, he says.

I try to laugh, but it comes out like a snort.

Why don't you believe it? I say.

I can see it in your eyes, he says. And moreover, you cannot conjure up love through conversation alone.

You have a point, I say, and feel uncertain about my adeptness at reading myself.

Sorte Firkant Café and Trabi Bar
Nørrebro Neighbourhood in Copenhagen
April 2017

We meet regularly at Sorte Firkant on Blågårdsplads but end up at Trabi Bar in Griffenfeldsgade after hours when both Sorte Firkant and Café Blågårds Apotek close up for the day. Niels is the one who brings us together. Sometimes there are six or eight of us, today only three in addition to Niels and myself: the musician who's part of the group Niels meets up with in the morning at Kaffesalonen before they continue on their way to work on their bikes, and the poet who Niels and I know from far back, as well as the Marxist art historian who Niels got to know when he was released from Vestre Prison.

Niels had been remanded by mistake and subsequently acquitted. He had participated in the demonstration against the demolition of the Youth House.[11] The whole wretched business ended up with the men becoming friends, and I revel in their revisiting of revolutionary ideas, of art, of gentleness, and their lucid conversations about anxiety and love's sorrows. And I succumb to laughter when the high-flown bubbles burst.

It's the Marxist art historian who does the bursting.

How's it going with the shooting of the *DirtyOldMan* programs, Niels? he says dryly.

Niels and I have just brought back some beer from the bar. Here we take turns getting bottled beer for the whole group. And it is taken for granted that those with the highest income go to the bar most frequently. As we set the bottles down on the table, the art historian looks up at Niels. And, as if he were asking Niels a question about his work, he inquires about the shootings of *DirtyOldMan*.

Niels cracks up.

What's that about? I ask.

Haven't you heard about the *DirtyOldMan* programs? says the art historian, with emphasis on *Old*.

The poet sits with his arms folded, shaking his head.

Niels wipes the laughing tears off his cheeks.

Well, I was chatting up this girl at my local bakery, he says, and then it turns out that she's only nineteen, and now it's become a thing for him over there.

Niels nods in the direction of the art historian, who's staring innocently at me.

The musician turns toward Niels with a grin.

Niels puts his hand on the musician's arm.

Thank you for a nice time yesterday, my friend, he says.

The musician nods.

What were you doing yesterday? I ask.

We went on one of our trips to my summer cottage, the musician says.

And I was dropped off at the local church, Niels says, where I sat contemplating while he was mowing the lawn.

Niels looks at the musician, who smiles back at him.

Niels is the only one in the group who uses churches for that sort of thing, and the art historian is about to say something but checks himself.

I also feel like placing my hand on the musician's arm. He and the churches and the intense, daily Messenger thread between Anne, Niels, and me help to suck the love anxiety out of Niels, who has just lost his girlfriend.

Later in the evening we're at Trabi Bar. The smoke is thick.

The poet gets up to go to the bathroom. The rest of us talk about women and losses.

The Marxist art historian doesn't participate in the conversation, he's bent over a mobile, concentrating, writing a message, I notice.

The poet returns. The mobile that the art historian just used dings. The poet picks it up. Apparently it's his. He looks startled, he cradles his head in his hands.

Fuck, fuck, fuck! he says, and starts typing away.

What's happening? I ask.

The poet doesn't answer, he's writing at a frenetic pace.

Everyone leans over the table. Except for the art historian, who's leaning back in his chair, his eyes twinkling and the corners of his mouth turned up in a little smile.

The poet lets go of the phone and rubs his face.

Ten years of trying hard to maintain a good relationship with my ex have just gone down the drain, he says.

What? the musician says.

He's been messing around on my mobile again, the poet says, nodding toward the art historian.

Niels shakes his head and says:

Again?

You people didn't keep an eye on him, the poet says, and looks at us accusingly.

The art historian follows the goings-on as if the conversation isn't about him.

The poet shows us the exchange with the ex-wife:

What's up, good-looking, feel like doing something dirty later?

What the hell are you talking about, you drunken bastard! Have ten years of trying to maintain a good relationship just gone down the drain?!

No! No! No! It wasn't me who wrote it!!! It was the art historian, again!

Phew, for a minute I thought...Keep an eye on your phone, please!

I look expectantly at Niels and the musician. They seem a bit uneasy.

Niels rubs his face with both hands.

Oh, you, he says, looking at the art historian. You're obviously raving mad.

Then he starts laughing.

The poet follows suit, doubles up with laughter. Slaps the art historian hard on his upper arm.

Be thankful that I love you so much, he says.

The Marxist art historian smiles at him.

Niels shakes his head and opens his arms.

This is fucking insane, he says.

When I'm back home and have thrown the smoke-soaked clothes in a pile on the floor, I sit down on my bed and write a message to Niels:

Thank you for a nice evening, Niels! Always great for me to be in the company of you and the others. Going to Stolpegård tomorrow—hoping it will be the last time. Are you ok?

Stolpegård Psychotherapy Centre
Vangede
Greater Copenhagen Area
April 2017

My BPD diagnosis has turned into the empty shell that's hanging on the coat rack by the front door. I slap it lightly when passing it. But there's no life left in the shell. It hangs dry and shrivelled up beside my leather jacket.

I've asked the psychiatrist to assess whether the diagnosis is still viable.

I put on the leather jacket and bike to Stolpegård.

The psychiatrist writes:

Progress report regarding therapy. Summary:
The patient has participated in six intro sessions, with good results, and has subsequently participated in group therapy once a week. After a short time she sees herself as having recovered, she feels well, and we have agreed to terminate the therapy.

Re: Borderline Personality Disorder:
She is described, and also describes herself, as being considerably stabilized. Describes herself as being able to

self-regulate, even in tense situations. She reports that she has been able to be without a boyfriend for the past eight months and that she functions well with that.

The diagnosis hardly qualifies any longer.

Suicide risk:
No thoughts or impulses, risk level 1

Frederiksberg and Nordvest Neighbourhoods in Copenhagen
May 2017

The doorbell rings, and I push the button to unlock the front door downstairs. I hear heavy steps coming up the stairs as I lean against the door frame, waiting to see who the person might be. A mailman carrying a cardboard box under his arm appears at the top of the staircase. He's breathing heavily and smiles at me.

You live in heaven, he says.

Yes and no, I say.

It's a long way up here, he adds, and hands me the box.

It contains my ten complimentary copies of an Irish novel I have translated. I place the box on the table and open it with a kitchen knife. I have my knives under control. I'm busy with the translations, their deadlines are close together, and during the short gaps between them I scramble to work on my own novel.

The sky is clear today, and the sun flows in through the big windows with the many panes, settling on the floor in patterns of limpid light: small squares separated by muntin bars at the top, large rectangles below. I close the curtains so I won't be blinded while I write at the dining table.

I write about seeing. I write about what vision means for writing.

Later on I get up from my chair. Several hours have passed since I last looked at the clock. I go into the kitchen to make coffee. While waiting for the water to boil, I open Tinder. I stand bent over the kitchen counter, resting on my forearms, swipe left a couple of times and feel almost nauseous.

But suddenly I straighten up. A physical awareness makes me do it. An awareness I haven't felt previously when I swiped. It's a tremor in my abdomen where a space has opened up, now that the anxiety beast has withdrawn.

Henrik is his name. He's two years older than me. He has narrow eyes, hair that's almost black, and an aquiline nose in a narrow face. He reminds me a bit of the Indigenous people that I adored in the old Westerns. Attraction is a hook that seizes on instinctual preferences.

But more than that, in the picture he doesn't seem to be putting on airs. He sits on a bench with his hands in his lap and smiles without looking self-conscious.

Like me, he has included a long profile where he describes what a good romantic relationship means to him. *I long for eyes that see me,* he writes, among other things.

I swipe to the right. There's a match.

Shortly after, I receive a long message from him. He doesn't write anything about what he thinks about my appearance. He comments on my profile, the part where I write about what a good relationship means to me. He writes that he feels we're similar. That our strengths and vulnerabilities are similar.

I ask if his body is calm or restless. He describes situations which cause him to feel restless.

I walk with Niels from Balders Plads in the Nørrebro neighbourhood. We walk around the lake in Utterslev Mose and end at Behov Pizzeria in the North West Block, where we eat pizza and drink wine. I sit close to Niels and show him the picture of Henrik and his profile on Tinder.

Niels concentrates as he reads it, scrolling the text along with his index finger.

He seems really great, Karen, he says.

Falernum Bistro
Værnedamsvej
Vesterbro Neighbourhood in Copenhagen
May 2017

I arrive before Henrik, stand in the middle of the room, and wait to be shown to the table I've reserved. After a short while I see him on the street. He's tall. Has straight posture. Walks stiffly.

It could turn out to be a long evening, I think. With that stiffness.

We walk to the table at the very back of the room. I feel like turning on my heel and leaving. He sits down on the tall bench. It's difficult for him to climb up, and I look on, skeptically. How the hell could I have been so mistaken about him, I think.

I've just had surgery, he says.

Ah, I say, and think that the stiffness might be caused by the surgery and not by a compression of his soul.

When the waiter arrives, Henrik speaks in a clear voice. He asks about the wine and the menu, laughs. When he laughs, his eyes turn into narrow cracks where nothing but reflected light is visible. I cannot help but smile in return. He leans his head back. A deep-throated laugh gushes out of his mouth.

The food and wine arrive. Not a bottle, a glass each. I had thought we should make do with a glass. So I could slip away quickly. He eats. Drinks like a man who's enjoying it. I drink, and my curiosity is piqued again. We order another glass.

He wears a ring in one of his ears. I look and I look. He takes off his jacket. On his forearm are two tattooed arrows, and a scorpion composed of small dark grey sections that winds itself around his upper arm.

I always sweat, he says. Have to bring an extra T-shirt and deodorant when I'm out dancing.

I've seen you before, I say, and nod toward the tattoo on his upper arm.

It hits me suddenly.

Where? he says.

In Underhuset, the club. You were soaking wet when you were dancing.

Then it was probably me, he says, and laughs.

I tell him about the time I stole a deodorant. I was seventeen and in Grade 11, and at the time I lived by myself in Kolding and made money as a dishwasher at Hotel Saxildhus, where I later hooked up with the trumpet player from Copenhagen. With the money I earned I bought cigarettes. So I decided to go down to Føtex and steal a deodorant. After all, the incident with the porn magazine had been successful several years earlier.

But at the exit I was stopped by a store detective and hauled all the way to the back of the supermarket, the man's hand clasped around my upper arm. Faces were turning in my direction. Soon I was inside a small room where cashiers were sitting with their packed lunches. In a desperate attempt to hide my all-consuming shame, I embarked on a long rant about cashiers' working conditions.

There had just been a strike in Føtex in Kolding. My father and several others from Kolding Højskole had been on the picket line trying to prevent the scabs from entering. I had already given up on the store detective, who was standing in the doorway keeping an eye on me while waiting for the police, but I gambled on winning over the cashiers to the revolution. Decent working conditions. The cashless society. But they went on chewing and stared at me, a lowlife. I stopped talking.

I don't think I've ever told this to anyone before, I say, and empty my glass.

Henrik gives me an affectionate look.

I've also stolen something from Føtex supermarket, he says. When I attended the Free Highschool, we lived in a commune nearby, and we didn't have any money either. So we stole from free-market capitalism. Føtex in Birkerød.

I love that he says free-market capitalism.

Two of us went inside and filled up two shopping carts. One with cheap items—toilet paper and that kind of thing. The other one with expensive things—meat, cold cuts. Then we wheeled the cart with meat out front to where vegetables are displayed and pretended to look for potatoes. Another couple of guys would race by on roller skates, grab the cart, and take off with it.

I take his hand. It's large. I don't do well with small hands and small dicks. I'm a cliché.

We're tipsy. Pay and stumble across the street and sit down outside Café Viggo. Begin drinking beer and smoking. The packet with Bali Shag tobacco moves back and forth between us. He rolls with experienced fingers. Gives his head a small toss when licking the paper. My fingers slowly remember how it's done.

I notice he's sitting with my purse and leather jacket in his lap. Don't remember how it all ended up there. There's a certain tenderness in the way his arm and hand hold on to my things.

I rest my head on his right shoulder. He lifts his right arm and stretches it to cradle my face. It stays there.

Look at the stars, a woman says to us.

And the colour of the sky, I say.

It's black tulip, Henrik says. My hair colour was like that the time I stole from free-market capitalism, he adds.

I kiss him. His lips are soft, his kiss is relaxed. I dig my fingers under the neckline of his shirt. His skin is warm. I feel his soft hair.

I want you, he says, and looks at my mouth. Very very much.

I want you very very much too, I say.

He pulls me close to him.

But listen, I say, we shouldn't be hammered the first time.

For once I don't feel I'm posing as an adult. I actually feel like an adult.

Shortly after, I get up on my bike and sail right through the intersection of Værnedamsvej and Gammel Kongevej.

Wow, I shout to him, afraid to turn my head. I just made it!

My Father's Funeral
Sønder Stenderup, Jutland
May 2005

Have I told you that you taught me how to see?

That you taught me to see the droplets from your nosebleed forming threads in your bowl of soured milk pudding like a spread of roots, slowly coalescing into shapes mimicking heart chambers? That you taught me to see the wind clawing at the glassy water, transforming foamy crests into furry, twitching tails?

That you have asked me to tell you what I see? Asked me to describe all the faces I saw. All the feet, hands, trees, birds, animals, all the rivers, mountains, roads that roll out like tongues throughout landscapes, the men, the skin, the books in your bookcases, the piped rivers of blood under men's skin.

As if you were blind.

Have I told you that you taught me to differentiate between various smells? When the honeysuckle emitted its threads of fragrance on summer nights. We had to walk on, we were in a hurry, there were so many smells and scents to explore. We would grasp cut-up logs with our hands and press our nose against the wood to soak up the smell of resin. We had to make time in October to smell the autumn rot in Swedish forests, sniff the seaweed by Nissum Bay and the stagnant water in the beach meadows' enlarged pores.

I shall smell male armpit sweat. Semen that runs down my thighs the morning after.

Have I told you that you taught me how to let sounds flow into my ears? How to distinguish different sounds and name them? The lark. That you showed me with your hand how he sits high above our heads, trembling and making the very sound that comes out of your mouth. That there are sounds in cresting waves and in trees, in snow and the grand piano, in the hymns.

That there are sounds in words: flesh, intonation and rye, sawtooth, paper and free-market capitalism.

That you taught me how to stretch my anxiety skin so it's no thicker than blotting paper that can absorp all sorts of things or let them bleed out? That you have taught me to see the cracks in the distended skin gauze, right there where whatever is underneath shines through? Right there where the non-face is. Right there where feet flip over and drag on their insteps. Right there where anxiety oozes out?

Have I told you that you're not the one who taught me how to taste and touch?

Have I told you that yesterday I saw the deep rectangular hole in which you're going to lie? And the dirt beside it that will cover you?

Have I told you that when we lowered your coffin today, I forgot what you shouted at me from below? When I was dangling at the top of the rope suspended from the copper beech and had to come down. It will burn if you let the rope slide through your hands, you shouted.

Have I told you that you gave me language?

Acknowledgements

Thank you to my editor, Julie Paludan-Müller, for having helped me get out of my lengthy writing crisis and for all her hard work in making it possible for this novel to find its shape.

Thank you to Simon Pasternak, my co-editor for a good part of the journey.

Thank you to my agent, Lars Ringhof.

Thank you to Mikkel Bogh, Anne-Cathrine Riebnitzsky, Lene Kaaberbøl, Monica Krogh Meyer, Jens Ulrich, and Lola Baidel for their financial backing, loans, and moral support while I was on sick leave.

Thank you to Helle Stavnem, Rolf Stavnem, and Sigrid Stavnem for finding me a place to live.

Thank you to my sister, Anne Fastrup, for reading freshly written text fragments on a weekly basis during various periods and for helping me out of the writing crisis. Thank you to my brother, Niels Fastrup, for also having read pieces in the course of the production and for having contributed, like Anne, with critical commentary. Thank you to both for being there and for supporting me while I was ill.

Thank you to my brother-in-law, Mikkel Bogh, not only for his financial support but also for putting me up and for his good, healing conversations.

Thank you to Ida Helene Asmussen for her friendship and for helping me out of my illness.

Thank you to my children, Malte Fastrup Lyngsø and Selma Fastrup Lyngsø. Thank you for being in the world and for all the things we do and have together, and thank you for having endured the period of my illness.

Thank you to Unit F3A (now Unit C231) at Frederiksberg Psychiatric Centre. A special thank you to Per Hansen and Gitte Skyggelund. Thank you to Stolpegård Psychotherapy Centre. Thank you to Line Hansen and Rune Stoltenberg Kristensen. Thank you to Anne Hansen and Allan Theland. Thank you to Susanne Feierskov.

After the publication of *Hungerhjerte* in Denmark, it was determined that the diagnosis of borderline personality disorder I received was incorrect. I then received the proper diagnosis of ADHD combined with anxiety and stress reactions. ADHD and borderline personality disorder are sometimes confused, especially in women.

A special thank you to Marina Allemano for the great work translating *Hunger Heart* and for allowing me into the process along the way. I appreciated her willingness to listen sensitively and tirelessly to my questions and comments, in particular regarding the translation of metaphors, linguistic images, and ambiguous layers that live in the voice of the narrator.

Also, a big thank you to Jay and Hazel Millar and everyone at Book*hug Press for publishing *Hunger Heart*. I am grateful and proud to have my work published by such an exquisite publishing house.

Notes

1   Askov Højskole and Kolding Højskole are two of the seventy Folk High Schools in Denmark, educational residential institutions located for the most part in rural areas or small towns. The schools provide a general broadening education (e.g., social studies, the humanities, nature studies, art, music, sports) and do not award marks or grades.

2   "benzodiazepines eat your soul" is a reference to Rainer Werner Fassbinder's film *Ali, Fear Eats the Soul* (*Angst essen Seele auf*, 1974).

3   The Danish line "Ved jorden at blive, det tjener dig bedst" (Keeping your feet on the ground will serve you best) is from one of N. F. S. Grundtvig's many patriotic songs, "Langt højere bjerge så vide på jord" (1820). Grundtvig (1783–1872) was a minister in the church, a poet, a historian, a politician, and the founding father of the Folk High School movement. The Danish landscape, the sense of community, and the people (or the folk) are prominent topoi in the song.

4   The Danish line "træd varsomt, thi scenen er skrå" (tread the boards with care, for the stage is sloped) refers to a popular Danish song from 1926 that warns young girls not to be blinded by the theatre's magic. In earlier times, theatres were designed with sloped (or raked) stages that could be challenging for actors and dancers to navigate.

5   *Det sultne hjerte* (2015) [The Hungry Heart] by Simon Kratholm Ankjærgaard, and *Personlighedsforstyrrelser. Moderne relationel forståelse og behandling af borderline-lidelse* (2009) [Personality Disorders: Modern Relational Understanding of Borderline Personality Disorder] by Carsten René Jørgensen.

6   "Livets veje" (1937) ["The Roads of Life"], a tale by Karen Blixen (also known by her pen name Isak Dinesen).

7   Kolding Højskole was established in 1972 and became a "red" centre for the progressive, anti-patriarchal, and anti-authoritarian movement in the Danish Folk High Schools.

8   The books referred to in this chapter are by Danish, Swedish, and Norwegian writers and considered "serious" literature, published between 1876 and 1968. By contrast, the books by the prolific Danish writer Ib Henrik Cavling are labelled "popular" or "light" literature. All the books mentioned have been translated into English except for *Vindane* [The Winds] by Tarjei Vessas, the two novels by Jakob Knudsen, and the novel *Charlotte* by Ib Henrik Cavling.

9   *Arv og Miljø* (2016), by Norwegian Vigdis Hjorth, was translated into Danish by Karen Fastrup (2017) and into English by Charlotte Barslund with the title *Will and Testament* (2019).

10   The quote is from Rainer Maria Rilke's *The Notebooks of Malte Laurids Brigge*, translated from German by Robert Vilain (Oxford World's Classics, Oxford UP, 2016).

11   Ungdomshuset [The Youth House], previously known as Folkets Hus [The People's House], has a long history as a gathering place for labour movements and left-wing groups and more recently as a hangout for squatters. In 2007 the building was cleared by the police and subsequently demolished.

About the Author

Danish author Karen Fastrup is the author of six novels. Her most recent book, *Hunger Heart* (*Hungerhjerte*), published in Denmark in 2018, was shortlisted for the DR's Novel Prize in 2019. The Danish Arts Foundation called the book "a work of particularly high artistic quality." *Femina Magazine* named Fastrup one of the seven most remarkable women in Denmark in 2019, and the year's "Taboo Breaker" for the awareness *Hunger Heart* created around mental illness. In addition to her own writing, Fastrup has translated more than fifty novels into Danish by such notable authors as Sally Rooney, Karl Ove Knausgård, August Strindberg, Linn Ullmann, Vigdis Hjorth, and Per Petterson. Her novel *Beloved of My Twenty-seven Senses* (tr. Tara Chace) was published by Book*hug Press in 2008. Fastrup lives in Copenhagen.